Also by Jonathan M. Cook

Youth and Other Fictions
The Sleep of Reason Produces Monsters

SINNERMAN
Jonathan M. Cook

This is a work of fiction. Names, characters, places, and incidents either are the product of the author's imagination or are used fictitiously, and any resemblance to actual persons, living or dead, business establishments, events, or locales is entirely coincidental.

SINNERMAN

Cover art and author photograph by Jonathan M. Cook

For Floyd Kryznowski and Richard Cook,
the gentlest of gentlemen.

I beg you, my brothers, do not act so wickedly. Behold, I have two daughters who have not known man; let me bring them out to you, and do to them as you please; only do nothing to these men, for they have come under the shelter of my roof.

-Genesis 19: 7-8

F. BARN.   Thou hast committed—
BAR.   Fornication—but that
           Was in another country: and besides,
           The wench is dead.

-Christopher Marlowe, *The Jew of Malta*

In a darkened room, the soft of her palms against my face. The damp pressure of her lips. A slight shudder as she curves her body against mine. A sigh as our lips part. Her hair like jet-black lilacs. Her skin like fresh baby powder.

Her dress falls to the floor. A black lace bra worn special against the white of her supple breasts. A slight bump at the center of either cup. Gooseflesh erupting across her flat, bare stomach, the small of her back. My tongue along the slope of her earlobe. Breathy utterances in some primordial language. Hands searching for a metal clasp. Release. The shock of chest against chest. The growing warmth spreading, engorging.

"Please," she manages. Eyes squeezed shut. The first tentative fumblings with button and zipper. A gasp. A radiating heat. A deepening slick.

"Please." Guiding hands.

"This is wrong."

"Please." Urging hands.

The inevitability of ecstasy.

Why didn't you tell me?

Chapter 1
Carry On Wayward Son

The idiot cleaned the tables with the dedication of a well-trained beast. He snaked through the dining area, weaving between tables, his arms hanging limp at his sides, his head turning to survey the room only after he ceased all other movement. When clearing a table, he stacked plates from largest to smallest, added silverware two pieces per layer, and then carried the whole pile with one hand while collecting a glass per finger with the other. On the occasions when he found himself lacking enough hands to carry everything, he would stand in place and stare at the table, as if confused and defeated by whatever remained. Then he would place everything back on the table, try to collect things in a more sensible manner, fail, and begin again. This would be repeated until one of the waitresses noticed and took over. And then the process would repeat itself at another table.

I watched the idiot do all this while sitting alone in Baba Yaga's Wing Hut with a half-eaten wrap and an empty beer glass in front of me. I was sitting alone because I worked as an English teacher in a tiny community where the chances of meeting someone were roughly the same as encountering the Jersey Devil while snowboarding in the Alps. I'd made my peace with it, though. Being alone has the consolation of not having to worry about anniversaries and other effluvia no one really cares about but which people always make a big deal over. Or the ridiculous exchange of gifts like payment for services rendered. Plus, a man can own a fire-engine red convertible and go tear-assing toward Vegas whenever the walls start closing in without feeling like a douchebag. Not a complete douchebag, anyway.

Besides, a man at the start of his career needs distractions the way the Japanese need lifts in their shoes. They might be nice initially, but long term, things like that always end up burning you. During my first year as a teacher, I had enough trouble figuring out why the paperclips were kept under guard in the main office and what the esoteric buttons on the copy machine control panel meant. Keeping a woman happy seemed trivial in comparison. My second year was easier, except for the administration completely changing my course assignments. I went from teaching seventy unruly freshmen to teaching seventy unruly sophomores. Same group, same problems, but at least I knew how to keep the copier from jamming.

Quite coincidentally, my sophomore year was also the year I met Elizabeth, a bank teller as eager to please as any young woman trapped in the middle of nowhere. Our liaison was productive only insofar as it provided a mild distraction from the tedium of the classroom. After only a matter of weeks, though, her intent to marry became too obvious to ignore. That is the trouble with dating in a small town: casual coupling is viewed as a pretext for something more substantive, despite the fact—or perhaps because of it—that this particular town found itself host to all manner of adulterous relationships. It was a well-known secret that several members of the managerial staff at the chocolate factory were closeted homosexuals who frequented Internet sites devoted to clandestine personal encounters. It was also understood that the vice president of the savings and loan selected a new mistress at the start of each fiscal year from amongst the personal bankers. Word was, this was the speediest method of career advancement, which came as a shock to no one but the evangelical congregation that met just outside the town limits. The minister of this same congregation was believed to have once carried on some kind of illicit relationship with the organist, though this was rarely accepted as gospel since both the organist and the minister were happily married and their families routinely attended church functions together.

Elizabeth and I came to end on a Sunday afternoon when she, in tears and desperate to gain control of the situation, cried pregnancy in order to goad me into a more permanent commitment. When I called her bluff, her tears came more freely and she said she wanted a child to love. I shrugged. I did not want a child and I certainly did not want to be with a woman who would resort to such pedestrian tactics to keep a man. Manipulation, as my father once told me, is not very fertile ground for a relationship.

The experience let me sour on relationships, though, and I spent that Christmas break roughing out a novel that never materialized. Though I was certain I had both a story to tell and a voice with which to tell it, I found myself offering nothing more than trite observations expressed much more profoundly by any number of writers before me. For all my effort, I returned to work at the end of the holiday with a single piece of paper upon which was typed a single word: "Fuck."

The school year continued and finally concluded with nothing of note occurring, save for the suicide of one of the janitors. His name was Gustav, an older man with a crooked back who enjoyed drinking coffee in the teacher's lounge and discussing the politics of thirty years ago. He was found in his garage with an extension cord wrapped around his neck. The school attempted to collect money for a bouquet of flowers to send to the funeral, but the union claimed such a request amounted to extortion, so the school sent nothing.

My third year teaching was more of the same: new course assignments, same group of students, but with the added joy of putting together that year's prom. In September, the junior class settled on "Casino Night" as that year's theme. In October, we locked in our DJ of choice. In November, we ordered a mass of cardboard decorations that came in flat boxes with no directions and insufficient tape. By January, we had everything well in hand, but February brought with it the realization that our class account had been almost totally depleted of its funds. As a result, we had to serve nothing but water at the dance—water without ice, because we had no money to pay for ice. The greater concern to the administration was our lack of proper headgear for the king and queen. This was solved through the use of a hot glue gun procured from the art department and a bucket of poker chips procured from my neighbor. Crowngate, however, paled in comparison to the t-shirt incident.

In order to encourage students to purchase their prom tickets in advance, the junior class offered a complementary t-shirt to the first two hundred students who purchased a ticket. The design of the shirts, chosen to go along with the post-prom party theme "Sailing Into the Night," bore the regrettable image of two well-dressed teenagers leaning against the railing of a ship at sea with the words "Let's Get Wet!" printed beneath them. Principal Hunter initially vetoed the design on the grounds that it suggested both sexuality and alcoholism, but she later rescinded her veto after a number of angry calls from parents who didn't see what the big deal was. The issue came to naught, however, when everyone realized there was no money to pay for t-shirts, either.

The prom went off without a hitch, though I later learned a small but vocal group of students took to Facebook and declaimed the decorations as being "as boring as that shit Mr. Sane teaches in class and gets so excited over." The original post eventually garnered 7000 likes and better than 200 comments, only one of which defended my involvement and that one only because I wrote it.

These same students appeared in my Composition courses the following year. Principal Hunter told me to consider it a promotion, that I was being given these courses and these students because she felt I had "a proven capability for preparing students through a vigorous and unapologetic curriculum," whatever that meant. I think God was using her to play a twisted joke on me, giving me the same students yet again. It wasn't that I didn't like these kids—I truly had grown fond of many of them; they were, after all, the class on which I cut my teeth. The problem was, they knew me and I knew them, and after three years, the only thing that had changed was how brazen they were. As freshmen, they had been afraid to even ask to use the restroom. As seniors, it wasn't uncommon for one of them to say, "I've gotta take a leak, Mr. Sane. I'll be back." If I told him to wait, the response would be "Dude, do you want me to whiz on your floor?" That kind of openness may be great for an athletic team, but not so much for a classroom. Had their frankness proven beneficial to their work, I could have taken it in stride.

They were, however, seniors in high school.

The assignment was simple enough: choose one of eleven short stories and write an interpretation based on one of the critical theories we had been discussing over the semester. For seniors receiving college credit, this should have been easy. They should have read each of the stories, consulted their notes to determine which theories connected best with each story, and gone from there. The essays I received, however, demonstrated a lack of even the most rudimentary understanding of the theories, to say nothing of the stories themselves. When not providing plot summaries so thorough I might as well have been reading the original works, the essays indulged in the nonsensical analysis of minutiae that postmodernists love and everyone else avoids. Example: "Atwood's story exemplifies feminist theory due to the near-complete female cast." A convent has a near-complete female cast, but that doesn't make it feminist. Also: "Because the boy doesn't get the girl in the end, he decides to give in and go gay." Nice try, but no. And my personal favorite: "It is true to the villagers, and therefore true to the story, even if it is not true in any real world way." That could have been profound had it been supported or even explained, but this particular student wrongly assumed saying things in an obtuse way made for perfectly acceptable analysis.

The kids had done very poorly, but they didn't want to hear about it. When I passed their papers back to them, the first thing I heard was "I want to know why I got a D. I worked really hard on this!" Not "What did I do wrong?" Not "Can we talk about this after class?" They didn't even wait until I was finished returning all of the papers before complaining. But in the land of the lotus-eaters, everyone is a princess, and small towns are no different. The sons and daughters of the prime movers held a privilege no one could deny them, and anyone who had the audacity to admit the truth was likely to find himself hauled before the school board on trumped up charges of checking out Dr. So-and-So's daughter's ass.

And the indignation at being called out on their laziness extended to the average Joes, as well, the children of the factory workers and the farmers and the retailers. Had senioritis descended like some biblical plague upon the tolerable and intolerable alike? Perhaps, but the downward spiral had begun back in September, and it had only gotten worse over the intervening months. Now, with the paltry four-day weekend they called Spring Break behind them and prom skulking ever closer, the belief that school had already ended was reaching epidemic extremes. Never mind the six weeks remaining on the academic calendar. Never mind the term paper and second literary analysis. Never mind those last few scholarship deadlines. School was out for summer.

The faculty only compounded the problem. Consensus was that the year had been particularly taxing due to a bizarrely misshapen calendar with fourteen weeks in the first semester and eighteen in the second, to say nothing of the scandalous departure of our beloved band director over a slight case of being drunk in class. More abstractly, there was a malaise wafting through halls and permeating the classrooms. No one could explain it, or even clearly identify what it was, but everyone felt it. It seemed everyone spent the first few weeks in January reviewing material that didn't need reviewing and assigning busy work for which we'd give points but never actually grade. Things that had to be graded were collected but put on shelves or in drawers and ignored for weeks at a time. Progress was made throughout the semester, as it always is, but slowly, ponderously.

We blamed the weather. A mild winter, cold but almost completely without snow, warmed into spring midway through March. Suddenly, every student went from overcoats and sweaters to short shorts and tank tops. Dress code violations began to outnumber tardies. "It's too nice to be inside" could be heard murmured in any classroom, from teacher and student alike.

Nevertheless, there were things that needed to be done. A number of the seniors were taking classes for which they would receive college credit at the year's end through the local community college. Between these classes and actual college courses taken during the summer, a student could conceivably finish his associate's degree before his first full day of college. As a result, the community college kept the high school curricula under close scrutiny to ensure they weren't awarding credit for substandard work. The dual-credit teachers were expected to adhere to stringent—though not unreasonable—syllabi and cover material comparable to the equivalent college course. The college had yet, in nine years of offering dual-credit, to audit any of the teachers, but still the threat loomed like some awkwardly lumbering goliath.

Composition, the class pairing with which I had been entrusted, was supposed to focus on preparing college freshmen for the rigors of college-level writing. The prescribed curriculum, however, focused on narrative and expository writing to the almost total exclusion of argumentation. One essay out of nine during the first class was meant to be an argument, and the major term paper during the second class was only an argument for a specific section; the rest was merely a regurgitation of facts culled from scholarly articles. The second class did provide an opportunity to study literature, but such study was entirely subordinated to the essays. This suited my students fine, as most of them refused to read anything deemed academic. Unfortunately for me, this meant I had to strike a balance between tedious writing instruction reviewing the thesis and organization of an essay and the monotony of hearing myself lecture on critical theory while the students slept at their desks.

Balance or no, nothing had sunk in; I was sure of that when I saw the average grade in all three sections was a low C. Were it not for the five- and ten-point gimme assignments scattered over the previous weeks, grades would not have been even that high.

I could have chastised them for their laziness and their indifference. I could have yelled at them to wake up and start taking their lives seriously. I could have called them out as a bunch of bums waiting in line with their hands out. I could have, and I probably should have, but I didn't. Instead, I sat down at my desk, leaned back, kicked my feet up, and said, "I already know all of this material. I have two degrees in this subject. I would like all of you to take advantage of my knowledge. However, entering an F

17

as your final grade is just as easy as entering an A. Frankly, it makes no difference to me. I already got my credit for this class."

They looked at me and I looked at them, and then I sent them to the restroom before they could figure out I was bluffing. Of course it made a difference to me. Of course I wanted to give them all high marks. The popular conception of teachers is that we enjoy inflicting stress and misery upon our students, that we relish the opportunity to make students ineligible for their extracurriculars and get off on failing them at the end of the semester. The truth is, no teacher worth a coffee mug of camel spit does that lightly, but there is a difference between a student who struggles and a student who simply expects nothing from himself. As unfashionable an idea as it may be, not every student can be saved.

And soon these students, these children, would graduate into the real world with all its horrors and responsibilities. Not that they were at all prepared for such a transition, but I suppose the same could have been said of my class all those years ago. But they were almost adults, able to register for the draft and buy lottery tickets and rent porn. Three that I knew of had already willingly signed up to fight and die in a foreign land—they all seemed ecstatic about the idea and couldn't figure out why the faculty had difficulty sharing their enthusiasm. At least one couple was engaged. Their wedding was scheduled for the July immediately after graduation. They'd been dating since their freshman year. Rumor had it she once gave him a handjob amongst the library stacks, so maybe it was love. And then there was the girl trying to date a 23-year-old on the sly. I found out when I caught them necking in a booth in the back of the Chinese restaurant. I did not, at any time, see his hand on her breast.

Kids grow up. They get hair in awkward places and discover sex isn't nearly as scary as their health classes claimed. They fall in love, marry, and have children of their own, and then the cycle starts over. It's all so simple. Never mind that better than half of their marriages would end in divorce or that any number of them would turn out to be gay. Never mind the financial hurdles of life in new millennium America.

What's life without a few challenges?

The idiot stood beside the table and stared at me. I stared right back.

"It's okay," Morgan said as she came up behind him. "I've got this one. You can go clean table twenty-four."

He twisted the rag in his hands. "But I need to clean this table. I have not cleaned it yet. I'm supposed to clean off every table when it's cleared." He spoke slowly, as if each word was a challenge not simply to say but to actually settle on.

Morgan offered me an embarrassed smile and then pointed at my empty beer glass. "He's still working on his drink. He's not ready to go yet. He might order another one or maybe some dessert. We don't want him to feel like we're kicking him out, right?"

The idiot shuffled his feet and turned his whole body to look at me before shuffling completely around and walking toward what I assumed was table twenty-four.

"Sorry," she said as he took up his rag and began to clean.

"He's been working here since before I started coming, which was four years ago, and he still doesn't understand when he's supposed to do his job."

"He has issues."

"Don't we all?"

"Be nice!" She gave me a look of faux exasperation and then pointed at my beer glass. "Want another?"

"Just a glass of water. And I'm always nice."

"You're nice to the girls."

"I'm a dirty old man."

"Please. You're a haircut older than me."

"And you have very long hair. Speaking of which, when are you going to take me home with you?"

"What does that have to do with my hair?"

"I don't know. I thought maybe I'd comb it and then braid it. Or just splay it out on your pillowcase right before I run my tongue up your—"

She laughed and spun away, flipping her hair in my face. Ah, sweet

Morgan. My Morgan. Morgan, who could guess my order based on the day of the week. Morgan, with the little girl at home and the scar on her left wrist. The child ensured I'd never actually do anything with her, but I tipped well and a bit of flirtation every now and then was harmless.

I picked up my pen, opened my notebook, and reread what I'd written before my meal:

A child looks out her bedroom window on her twenty-fifth birthday and takes in the cruelty of a thunderstorm that began, depending on one's perspective, late last night or early this morning. Either way, it is not weather a young woman of any breeding should be out in, save for the most pressing of business, which explains why, after returning the curtains to their original position and checking that the pearls dangling from her ears match the pearls surrounding her neck, the child selects from her closet a hooded full-length cloak of dark purple velvet. This she wraps around her slight frame and secures at the neck with a simple gold clasp. Her dark brown hair she pulls back into a crude ponytail and fastens with a black hair tie.

Before leaving, she pauses to gaze wistfully at a framed photograph atop her dresser. The photograph depicts a man and a woman, neither many years older than her, standing side by side. The man is full in the face, with grey eyes and a curious patch of hair beneath his lower lip that would have been called, during its short period of prominence, a soul patch. He stands as much as a foot taller than his companion. The woman is very pale, so much so that her black hair clashes almost violently against her skin. Her small brown eyes sit at odds with her pronounced Italian nose and her thin mouth. There is nothing within the frame to clarify their relationship, if indeed any relationship existed. The expression on the woman's face is one of girlish euphoria, while the man's sobriety borders on a grimace, as though the act of having his picture taken caused him physical discomfort.

The child reaches out to stroke the glass with index and middle fingers, stops, and instead draws her hand against her neck. Her thoughts are her own, and whatever the significance of the photograph, she remains silent. She is alone.

"And why do we care?" I asked as I crossed out the last sentence.

Morgan returned with a glass of water and the bill, which she placed to the side of my notebook and facedown.

"Read this for me," I said as I picked up the bill and slid my notebook toward the edge of the table.

She leaned over, holding the back of my chair and tapping the base of my neck with her thumb as she read. Finally, she straightened up and shifted her hips. "It's beautifully written."

"Yes, but as the audience, what's your response to what is written?"

"I want to know where she's going and who the people in the photograph are."

"She's going to an auction house to bid on a book manuscript."

Her eyes tightened and she bit her lower lip before bursting out in laughter.

"You're laughing."

She managed to calm herself and wiped at the corners of her eyes. "I'm sorry. It's not... I don't know anything about auctions and I know even less about book collecting."

"So you wouldn't read it."

"I'm not saying that. I mean, I might read it. But that's a different world for most people. People read what they can understand. You need something familiar to capture people before taking them to an auction."

"Sounds reasonable." I tore the page from the notebook and crumpled it into a ball. "Would you please incinerate this for me?"

Morgan took the wad of paper with a smile. It wasn't a particularly beautiful smile because she wasn't a particularly beautiful woman, but it was a sincere smile from a sincere woman, and that's what I liked about her. In a restaurant routinely packed with community college students and blue collars, Morgan acted as a perfect equalizer. It didn't matter how a person came into the restaurant, whether his clothes were ratty or fresh, whether he was old and decrepit or young and wet. He was treated the same as everyone else. She liked her job and she liked her customers, and I loved her for that.

On my way home, I came upon a truck on its side in a ditch with a woman sitting in the grass nearby with two dogs. I pulled over and asked if she was okay, but all she would say was that she was in big trouble. "I've done it this time, I've really done it," she kept repeating. I walked to the truck and peered through the windshield. There was no one inside. I asked the woman how she got out of the truck, but she ignored me. I pulled out my cell phone and called 911. As soon as I hung up, the woman started screaming for Don. "Don, I'm so sorry! Oh, Don!" When asked who Don was, she said he was her husband and that he was going to be so mad at her. After some prodding, I managed to get a phone number from her.

"What?" the man who answered shouted.

"Is this Don?"

"Who the hell is this?!"

"My name is Julian. I'm here with your wife. It looks like she ran off the road."

"I ain't married no more! She ain't my problem!"

"Well, she kept calling your name."

"Whadya want me to do about it?"

In front of my mirror that night, after I brushed and stripped down according to my nightly ritual, I heard Don's voice. He stared back at me from the glass, his ice blue eyes beneath a shaggy head of brown hair graying slightly at his temples, his biceps and upper chest softening. I could almost see him dropping from six feet to five, and though his lips never once moved, I kept hearing his voice: *Whadya want me to do about it?*

22

Chapter 2
Pretty When You Cry

The Friday before graduation, I sought out a piece of fresh fruit in the main office.

The main office, like the rest of the school, was a sterile amalgamation of light gray cabinets and dark gray speckled countertops. The main doorway led to a waiting area and a reception desk. Behind the reception desk was a short hallway flanked on other side by the administration offices and terminated by a conference room just big enough for a long table with twelve chairs. To the left of the reception desk was a door leading to the mailroom/office lounge. Taped to the door by all four corners was a piece of paper, on which in big, friendly letters was typed DON'T STEAL OFFICE FRUIT.

The secretaries always kept a stash in their fridge—something about the vitamin C offsetting the stresses of their toils—and picking through apples seemed to me a better way of spending the afternoon than counting tiles in the ceiling of my classroom again.

The fridge stood on the wall opposite the mailboxes, which meant anyone picking up his mail could sneak a piece of fruit without having to contribute to the fruit fund. It also meant that anyone picking up his mail was likely to turn around and find someone's ass sticking up in the air as the unfortunate bastard rooted around in the back for the best pieces. A petition to force the fridge's movement to another, less awkward location was frequently discussed, but every teacher in the building knew the cardinal rule of education: never fuck with the secretaries.

My search for an apple that day led Miss Connors, a PE teacher who somehow landed the coveted fifth period prep, to clear her throat and tap an athletic equipment catalog on my ass.

"What are you doing?" she asked.

I found an apple that met my basic requirements—golden green and firm all the way around with no brown spots—and withdrew from the chilly interior. "Taking a shower," I said. "It only looks like I'm searching for a piece of fruit."

She crossed her arms. "No, I mean, don't you have class right now?"

"Yes. Yes, I do. I should probably get back there. Wait, no, damn, I have nothing but seniors this semester."

Seniors were released from classes a week before graduation, which gave any teacher fortunate enough to have seniors a single protracted prep period for the rest of the year. The only downside was that we were expected—meaning required—to attend graduation.

"Oh, so you're basically done then."

"Yep. I probably need to clean the whiteboard, but other than that, I can sit around and wait for death. And get paid for it."

She laughed the harsh laughter of one who is trying way too hard. "That's funny."

"Isn't it?"

"Hey, I was wondering, are you seeing anyone right now?"

Oh dear god. "You mean, other than yourself?"

Her face pinched, as if considering whether that was a serious response. "I mean, are you dating anyone right now?"

"Ah! I get it. Damn precision language! No, at this moment, I'm actually eating an apple and talking with you, but I currently do not have a girlfriend, if that's what you're asking."

"Oh, okay."

"Why do you ask?"

In deference to decades of feminine coyness, she bit her lip and lowered her eyes. "I thought maybe if you didn't have any plans tonight, we could get some dinner together. If you don't have plans, that is."

Allison Connors. Petite Allison with the muscular arms and the A-cup breasts. Silly, girlish Allison, who knew as much about seducing men as she knew about particle physics and whose over-caffeinated personality might have been endearing if not for the Chanel No. 5 in which she bathed.

I took a bite out of my apple and considered my options. I did have a gig at The Disintegration Room that night, which was a convenient excuse not to spend time with her, but I was scheduled to go on at 8, which meant I'd be done by 9 at the latest, and with nothing else to do, I'd settle in for a night of heavy drinking. The Disintegration Room was technically within the town limits, which meant there was a chance, however slim, that I'd run into one of my students, so I'd have to go to one of the more costly bars in the surrounding area. Making dinner plans would probably end up costing less, given her thinness, but the food would dilute any alcohol consumed, lessening the chance for a happy ending to the night. More pragmatically, her effervescence would make the usual first-date conversations all the more intolerable, which would lead to heavy drinking on my part, which would lead to an inability to drive home safely, which would lead to her offering to drive me home. No woman drives me anywhere.

"Yeah, I really don't think so. We've barely spoken more than a dozen sentences to each other since you started last year and that leads me to believe you're less interested in getting to know me as a person than in having some hot teacher-on-teacher action, perhaps with some spicy student-teacher role-playing, which I am not opposed to—I have no problem with being nothing more than a piece of meat—but were we to have a sexual encounter, you would want more, you would need more, because I am very, very good in bed and I really focus on my lover's needs, but long term, what starts out as friends-with-benefits will become a relationship in which we've grown fond of each other, maybe it won't be love but certainly a kind of affection, and this will lead to talk of marriage and children and we'll go for it because why not, and soon we're both old and decrepit with plumbing that no longer works properly and we'll look at our lives and wonder how the hell we got here, and I really don't think that's what either of us want at this time."

Every cad knows the secret to seducing a woman, whether a timid virgin or a true nymphomaniac, is to shove her aside and make a great show of disinterest. Thanks to the conditioning powers of *Cosmopolitan*, women treat rejection as a significant blow to their self-esteem. Not even AstroGlide is a better lubricant.

Miss Connors took a step back, her eyes shrink-wrapped in the horror of a deer that knows its hunter is about to win. "I didn't mean anything, I was just asking to ask, we don't have to get dinner, it's, it's fine, really, I'm sorry, I didn't mean—"

And there it was: the subtle quickening of her breathing, the slight reddening of her cheeks, the dilation of her pupils.

I advanced on her even as she took a step back and I took another step forward and she pressed her back against the mailboxes. I rested an arm beside her and leaned forward to establish the power differential advertisers have relied on for years. "I'll tell you what: I've got a gig at The Disintegration Room tonight at 8. You come for the show and then we'll not get dinner afterwards. Sound good?"

She nodded.

"And take your B vitamins. You're going to need them."

With that settled, I pushed away from the mailboxes and headed back to my classroom, savoring my apple as I walked.

As I walked past the administration hallway, I heard the aged but still potent voice of Principal Hunter. "Sane! Get in here!"

"Boss?" I asked from her office doorway.

"You harassing the help again?"

I crossed my arms and gave my best wide-eyed-and-confused look. "What? When have I ever harassed the help?"

"Don't shit where you eat, Julian."

"Wouldn't dream of it, Maddy. Is that all?"

Principal Hunter removed her glasses and motioned at a chair in front of her desk. "No. Sit down. Are you ready for tomorrow night?"

Ah, yes. The graduation ceremony, meaning an interruption to my early summer vacation. "I need to iron my good underwear, but otherwise, I think so."

"You know they won't remember where they're supposed to go, so you'll be expected to lead them to their chairs and ensure they're all positioned properly."

Because we churn out nothing but the finest minds in America, and America does not expect its fine minds to be able to do anything so complicated as find a chair. "Cheryl and I go with the valedictorians to the dais. I don't get to lead anyone anywhere. That's why I went into teaching."

"Shit." She scratched at her lower lip with the arm of her glasses and looked genuinely perplexed at the implications.

"You nervous?" I asked, wanting the conversation to be finished.

"Graduation always makes me nervous."

"And how many years have you been doing this?" Since the first apes decided walking upright might be a nice change of pace?

"Watch it, kid."

"Relax, Maddy. There'll only be so many open seats. They'll have to sit in them. I think even this group can figure that out." Provided we have directional markers every few feet.

"I hope so."

I sat down. "What do you care? You're almost done. One more year."

"You'd be surprised how fast a storm can brew."

"Over graduation?"

"For some of these kids, this will be as good as it gets."

"That's just sad."

"Doesn't change how seriously their parents take it. You wouldn't believe the things I've gotten calls over. Air horns, for God's sake!"

"God bless the beautiful people."

"And God save the rest of us." Principal Hunter picked up a pen, opened a folder, and began filling out what I assumed was some kind of IEP form, apparently forgetting about me in the process.

That was the purest distillation of the education system. One problem solved only led into the next. One crisis averted only made room for another. Not that graduation was any kind of crisis, but the parents could easily make it so with their micromanagement. Some of those people still thought of their teenage years as the best of their lives and now having teenagers themselves gave them a chance to relive their golden age. Shit. Was adulthood really so bad? Was having to take responsibility for their own existence really that much of a pain in the ass? Yes, the economy was on the verge of total collapse and, yes, one's job was perpetually teetering over the edge of a cliff, but why was that a bad thing? Where was the perverse thrill of living in the shadow of an ending? We were the children of the millennium, God's own chosen to watch the coming apocalypse. Just ask the evangelists on television who kept demanding everyone repent and make ready the way of the Lord. Then again, what kind of god, Jewish or Greek or Sumerian, was going to come to rapture a handful of assholes who claimed to speak for it?

Those trapped in the middle, like poor Principal Hunter, didn't have the luxury of metaphysics. For them, the reality of John Q. Public's rampant ignorance was an all-encompassing distraction. Everyone knew better than the professionals. Everyone was convinced their children were above average. The bell curve was so far over their damned heads most couldn't even say the concept, let alone explain it. Eight hours a day of lecture and discussion and experimentation periodically interrupted with phone calls demanding justification and reconsideration and supplication.

I rose grateful that at the end of the summer, I would have tenure and would never need to placate anyone else who felt the television could do my job.

The Disintegration Room occupied the remains of a deserted convenience store, a studio building with the bar at one end and the stage at the other. It was, according to the factory workers, a fine place to forget the horrors of the assembly line. I could empathize.

"So she gets up during dessert to use the bathroom. Nothing unusual, nothing to be worried about. No hint that things are about to go very, very wrong. Well, she leaves her purse on the table. I don't know why. I mean, women always seem so attached to those stupid things, like they're a third tit or something. Anyway, so the waiter walks by and snags the strap and knocks it off the table. I'm a nice guy, I'm a gentleman, so I bend over to pick it up. Unfortunately, it's one of those purses without a zipper, so some of the contents spill out. You know, the usual items. Eye shadow. Mascara. Heavy-duty tampons. Ribbed condoms. And of course that's the moment she decides to return from the bathroom, with me on the floor rummaging through her purse. I try and tell her it's not what it looks like, but she takes the purse and proceeds to beat me over the head with it and scream that I'm a pervert, how could I, blah blah blah."

The drunks began laughing, either unaware of the lack of a punch line or too drunk to care.

"And I got stuck with the check, surprise surprise. That's what really pissed me off. Not that I wouldn't be getting a happy ending, but that the bitch had the audacity to stick me with the bill. What. The. Fuck. But at least I got some free condoms and tampons."

The laughter grew. One of them began slamming a beer mug on the countertop and others followed suit. Soon the entire bar was a cacophony of ringing glass. Those idiots would have laughed at a chicken laying an egg while Phillip Glass provided the score. Not once in the seven months I'd been performing had I told a joke that any real comedian would have considered a success. Garbo, the barkeeper and owner, seemed not to mind and kept inviting me back month after month. He also paid cash, which helped.

"Well, you drunken reprobates have been fun, but I think my hour's up, so please tip your waitresses and enjoy the rest of your livers. Before I go, though, does anyone have any cocaine for sale?"

More laughter.

"No, seriously. My date for the evening seems to have enjoyed the show, but there's always the possibility I'll fuck things up and be forced to go home to a very accommodating left hand, so if anyone has any coke to take the sting out of failure, you know, see me backstage. Thank you and goodnight!"

Applause reverberated throughout the room. From the barflys. From

Miss Connors. Even from Garbo, who normally was too busy spit-shining glasses during the acts. I clipped the microphone to its stand and hopped off stage. Miss Connors rose as I walked past her table. I motioned with my index and middle fingers for her to follow me to the bar.

Garbo nodded from the opposite end. "Have a drink. I'll be down in a minute."

His assistant, a petite blonde wearing a black bra and a short denim skirt—Garbo's standard uniform—wiped down the space in front of us and tossed the rag out of sight. "What can I get you two?"

"Allison?"

"I'll have a white wine spritzer," she said with what could only be described as a sorority slut's grin of vapid glee.

"And you?"

I'll need a minute while I decide whether I actually want to have sex tonight or rewire my house's Ethernet network. "Lagavulin. Double."

The blonde nodded and set an old-fashioned glass filled with ice on the bar. Before I knew it, she was pouring the Scotch over the ice.

"Whoa whoa whoa whoa! What the hell are you doing?"

She stopped pouring, thankfully. "I'm… getting your drink?"

"Do I look like I suck dick?"

"What?"

"Do I look like I suck dick?"

"No."

"Do I look like an asshole?"

"What?"

"Do I look like a fucking asshole?"

"No."

"Put down the Scotch and step away from the bar immediately."

Garbo came over and laid a hand on her shoulder. "S'okay, sweetie. I got it."

The three of us watched her sulk to the other end of the bar, casting glances over her shoulder at us as she did.

"Did ya have to be such a dick to her?" Garbo asked. "It's her first night."

I picked up the glass and held it between us. "See this? Do you see what she was doing to the Scotch?"

"Most people don't care if their Scotch's on the rocks."

I dumped the ice on the floor. "Most people also think Johnnie Walker is an acceptable Scotch. That doesn't make them right."

"Fine. One Lagavulin. Double. Neat. And for you, miss?"

"For reasons surpassing understanding, the lady would like a white wine spritzer. I'd also like my payment, please."

Garbo grunted but set to mixing Miss Connors' spritzer without further comment. I poured the Lagavulin and then held the glass to the light to examine the amber hue for any melted ice pollutants. After Garbo finished with the spritzer, he reached into his pocket and pulled out a wad of bills. He peeled off three fifties and laid them folded beside my Scotch.

I tapped the pile. "Tut tut tut. This is not my usual payment."

He placed his hands on his hips. "Yer drinks—"

"—are the cost of doing business." I tapped the pile again.

"Ya really are an asshole, Sane," he said as he laid down another fifty.

"I love you, too, Garbo," I said, collecting the bills.

The barkeeper made a gesture both obscene and unnecessary, given the mixed company, and then moved onto bilking the drunks out of their union-earned wages. Miss Connors' stare was fixed on her drink and she stirred her spritzer with a red micro-straw, agitating the bubbles and causing a thin layer of foam to appear near the top of the glass. She kept doing this, not drinking or talking or even looking away. I sipped my Scotch.

"You think that was unnecessary," I said.

The straw slipped from her fingers, sank in the glass, and then buoyed back up on the carbonation. She shook her head. "No."

"No?"

"You didn't say you wanted ice."

"I also didn't say I didn't want ice, either."

"I guess."

"It was unnecessary. It was unnecessary and it was an overreaction and any other woman would have made up some excuse about needing to be up early tomorrow or needing to wash her hair, which confirms my earlier suspicion that you are only in this for my body, so what say you and I retire to one of the cramped little washrooms and find a simpler way of amusing ourselves?"

She blushed and gave a harsh, breathy laugh.

"Your pupils are dilated." I couldn't actually tell in the dim light of the bar, but it seemed a reasonable guess. "Pupillary dilation is indicative of increased interest in another person, or more specifically, of increased arousal. Would you like me to tell you the other physiological signs of arousal?"

I brushed a few strands of hair away from her eyes, grazing my fingertips against her forehead.

A single light bulb hung overhead, casting parts of the washroom in a sickly yellow light and other parts in deep, sharp shadows. The floor was sticky with vomit or urine or beer. Parts of the walls were caked with rust and water stains. The single stall door hung crooked from its hinges and wouldn't close without leaving a two-inch gap for eager onlookers. The usual off-color jokes, phone numbers, and penis drawings had been written on or scratched into the paint surrounding the urinal. The cake had long before been reduced to an empty plastic mesh frame. The sink was cracked in several places and water dripped onto the floor whenever the sink was active. The mirror appeared to have made contact with someone's head or fist and I had to hold onto the back of her head to keep her from cutting herself on the jagged lines.

There's no lock, I thought as I came. *There's no lock on the door.* And then: *I really hope none of my students come here.*

With my sleeve rolled up and the cuff inflated, I wondered where all the pretty nurses had disappeared to. When I was young, all doctors were assisted by pretty nurses, thin women in their twenties and thirties with long hair tied back into simple ponytails. They'd smile and tell me to relax and I would because their smiles made me feel warm in all the right places.

This one, though, instilled no such warmth. She instilled no desire, no fleeting fantasy. This one looked like she'd eaten her last patient and still had room for a second helping.

She pumped the bulb and the cuff tightened. And tightened. And tightened.

"This is my dominant arm, so I'd like for it to not fall off before you finish, if that's possible."

The cuff tightened further. "Don't talk."

The cuff slowly deflated. "Blood pressure's elevated."

"How high?"

"It's elevated. Are you nervous?"

"No. Should I be? Do I have cancer? Am I going to die soon?"

The nurse draped the sphygmomanometer around her neck, made a note in my file, and then closed it. "The doctor'll be in shortly."

"Do I have that long?" I tried my best to sound irritatingly worried, but the nurse just walked away.

Forty-five minutes and three issues of *Highlights* later, Dr. Louise Samson brought her petite frame, C-cup breasts, and flowing mane of blonde hair to my room.

"Good morning, Julian," she said. "How are we feeling today?"

"I'm good, doc. Thanks. And thanks for seeing me on a Saturday. I know it's not real convenient for you."

She opened my file and began to read. "I have to be here anyway, so I figured I could fit you in."

"I love it when a beautiful woman fits me in."

"Oh, that's so sweet! Let's start with the prostate exam."

I held up my hands in mock defeat. "Point taken. I should not be flirting with my doctor and I feel deeply, deeply ashamed."

She ignored me. "Your blood pressure is a bit high."

"So I heard."

"You under any excessive stress lately?"

"No, no more than usual."

"Still teaching?"

"Yeah. Think I should quit?"

"No. It'll keep you young."

"Really?"

"No, it's just something we say to teachers. Takes the sting out of having a shitty job."

"Ouch."

"Take your shirt off."

She poked, prodded, groped, fondled, caressed, and kneaded my body in a variety of humiliating, yet strangely pleasant, ways for the next thirty minutes.

"You need to start taking care of yourself, Julian," she said as she pulled off the latex gloves smeared with lubricant and other stuff. "Your blood pressure is higher than I'd like it to be, you've put on weight, and your diet sounds like it leaves something to be desired."

"I eat just fine."

"Alcohol is not a food group. Nor is pizza."

"So I like my pies, so what? And I really don't drink that much."

"One a week?"

"Yeah. One a week."

"One a week?"

"Yeah."

"Julian, one what a week?"

"One bottle a week. That's not overdoing it."

"Julian!"

I hate when people pronounce my name like that: JOO-lee-annnnn. That's only acceptable when the person saying it is in my immediate family.

"Fine, doc! Fine! What do you want me to do?"

"Go easy on the booze."

. . .

"Start eating well-balanced meals."

. . . "Go on."

"Get some exercise every day."

Ah! I jabbed my finger at her. "I exercise plenty!"

"Real exercise. Walking the school does not count."

"I ain't talking about walking the school. Oh yeah, you know what I mean. Up high! Actually, that reminds me: I need an STD panel."

"Julian!"

"Hey, don't start! I am not kosher with spreading disease! Actually, I'm even less kosher with having any kind of disease, especially in my nether region! You should be applauding me for being socially responsible."

Dr. Samson put her hands to her temples. "Julian, I'm going to make this simple. If you don't start taking care of yourself, you won't have to worry about disease, because little Julian won't be able to lift his own weight. Do you understand?"

"This is why no one likes doctors. We come to you at our most vulnerable and all you do is humiliate us. Thanks a lot."

At this point, she finally snapped and slapped my file across my face.

"Feel better now?" I asked.

She took a pen from her lab coat. "Any particular STDs or should we just test for everything and hope we get lucky?"

"I'm feeling saucy, doc. Let's do it all."

She rose and went to the door. "I'll be right back."

When she returned, she brought her nurse, a needle, several vacutainers, and what looked like a cotton swab in a test tube.

"In order to ensure the validity of the test results, we're going to need a swab," Dr. Samson said.

… "Of what?"

"Drop your drawers, Julian."

Fuck.

Chapter 3
Champagne Supernova

The graduates assembled in the cafeteria an hour prior to the ceremony. I was tasked by one of the guidance counselors to ensure the boys' ties were photogenic and their cords were straight. After fixing fifteen or sixteen, though, I had to wonder how any boy in the twenty-first century could reach his high school graduation without knowing how to properly handle his own tie.

They congregated in groups of four or five or six and snapped photos on their phones and hugged like this was the end of the world, which I suppose it was for many of them. How many of my classmates did I still talk to even a month after graduation? There was Sam, but that was only because he was constantly screwed up and subsequently fun to laugh at. The rest of them I didn't give a damn for when I had to interact with them, and I certainly didn't like them any more post graduation. But my class, owing to the six feeder schools, had also been three times the size of this group. This group of 112 had been together, with the odd addition and subtraction, for twelve straight years. That kind of togetherness isn't healthy, but it does breed cohesion.

Hipster and jock. Black and white. Rich and poor. For one glorious night, neither clique nor race nor social status mattered. Prior offenses were forgotten, if not forgiven. Even little Heather Thomas seemed to bond with Jessica Finch, who had once covered Heather's Jeep with two hundred maxi pads as a misguided prank. No one labored under the illusion that any of this would last, but for the moment, they grew up. They actually were the adults we were about to christen them. I almost regretted writing what I had written for the senior goodbye in the school newspaper:

> During triumphal processions, a Roman emperor would be accompanied by a servant or a slave who would whisper in his ear, "Remember that you are a man." This served as a reminder to the emperor that no matter how great his accomplishments or how loved his reign, he would one day be nothing more than dust and bones.
>
> Though there is great joy to be found in your upcoming graduation, and though you should feel a certain elation, a tightening of your chests and a swelling of your hearts, there is also great sobriety to be found. You are now adults, masters of your own destinies. Upon receipt of your diplomas, you will be accepting total responsibility for your lives. For many of you, this means you will lose your safety nets, those people on whom you have come to rely for guidance and assistance. These people will still be around for some time, if you are lucky, but as friends, as colleagues, as neighbors. They will no longer be mentors.
>
> What comes next is hard. There will be anxieties over careers and money and love and family. There will be moments of profound loneliness and deep uncertainty. The floor will disappear from beneath your feet on more than one occasion and drop you into unfamiliar territory.
>
> How could it be any other way?
>
> But there is also triumph in standing on your own two feet. According to one poet, a man fleeing the destruction of his home founded Rome. He wandered and he suffered, often

sacrificing his own happiness for a greater good, and yet the culture he founded went on to become the most glorious of its time… and its glory persists even now, over a thousand years later.

Time is fleeting. In the end, we have precious few decades during which to leave some kind of marker that we were here. Will you leave a city that will endure for a thousand years? Will you leave an epic poem about the afterlife that will become a cornerstone of western literature? Will you leave a religion dedicated to a love of humanity? Will you leave a bloodline from which will come kings and presidents?

As you cross the stage to receive your diplomas and accept the congratulations of the administration, the faculty, and the board, remember that you, too, are human, and consider what you do with your life and what you will leave when you are gone.

The pragmatist in me said I was simply being honest, but the small corner of my heart that still clung like a barnacle to idealism wanted to believe they would succeed, that they would achieve in the way my generation had failed, that they would live the American dream. Nelson, who went through women almost as fast I did, would find true love. Renee, who had a panic attack upon receiving a B on one of her essays, would learn to relax. Even Alex, who felt the best he could do with his life was become cannon fodder, would come home from the Middle East a war hero. God, Zeus, Allah, or Whoever would bless the Class of 2012 and the world would be better for it.

Moreover, I held a genuine hope that these Millennials might prove capable of shedding my generation's callous indifference, that they would all grow into better men and women than me and mine. They might not be able to reverse or even stop the downward slide of modern America, but they would try. They would stop bickering over the details and make a concerted effort to change things. They wouldn't sit in darkness and drink their lives away. They wouldn't search for meaning in one-night stands.

The timid voice of Ashley Park broke my reverie. "Mr. Sane?"

I turned to face the boy with the girl's name and the wickedly unkempt head of hair. "Hey, Ashley. How are you doing? Ready for this?"

He was fidgeting, bouncing from foot to foot as though he really had to urinate. "Are you going to be here later?"

"Tonight? Yeah, I'll be around for a little bit."

"Can I talk to you afterwards?"

"Sure. Everything okay?"

"It can wait."

"Okay. Yeah, come find me after the ceremony."

He muttered "thanks" before being assimilated into a mass of sapphire blue gowns. I should have followed him and pressed harder, because in the four years I'd known him, Ashley had never been that visibly uncomfortable, but Jeff Moon was lifting the back of Michelle Crosby's gown to see where she kept her secrets and I had to intervene, even though most of the senior class already knew. By the time I disarmed the situation, Principal Hunter was mounting a table to deliver last minute instructions.

"Form up. Two lines, just like at practice. Make sure the person in front of you and the person behind you are the same as at practice. Mr. Sane will lead the first line and Mrs. Hyde the second. Follow them to the gym. Do not talk on the way there. Do not talk on the way in. Do not talk at your seats. Do not sit until directed to do so. Any questions?"

I donned my hood, which another member of the faculty insisted on tying to the topmost button of my shirt, found the arm slits, and clasped my right wrist in front of my stomach, assuming what I hoped was a pose of reverential solemnity but which probably just looked stupid to the graduates. Mrs. Hyde stood beside me and Bradley Allen stood behind me.

"Mr. Sane?" Bradley asked as the rest of the graduates assembled. "I think there's something wrong with your sleeves."

"It's a master's gown, Brad."

"Yeah, but your sleeves are falling out."

"That's where I stashed my peanuts."

"Really?"

"No, Brad, not really. It's a way of distinguishing it from the lesser gowns."

My stomach began growling at the thought of a salty snack, so I casually made my way toward the entrance of the cafeteria, where the vending machines were located, but someone had turned them off for the weekend, so all I could do was stare hopelessly at the sacks of expired peanuts.

The inward procession was marred only by one of the junior ushers being unsure how to get from the back of the gym to the dais and choosing to sneak behind a set of bleachers, only to catch a heel on a support beam and stumble into the dais rather ungracefully. The band played on and the only people who seemed to notice were members of the faculty, several of whom laughed out loud in relief that they were not the ones to mess up.

After a rousing welcome from the class treasurer, who took the opportunity to remind those in attendance about his full academic ride to Juilliard, Principal Hunter introduced the members of the school board, each rising for a brief applause as his or her name was called. Then came the valedictorian speeches. All nine of them.

Vespers Community High School's student handbook explicitly stated that the selection of valedictorian

> shall be determined on the basis of academic performance during the years of secondary education. Upon graduation, the student with the highest grade point average in his or her class shall be awarded this distinction with honors. In the event two or more students graduate with equal grade point averages, a full academic review of the qualifying students' records will be conducted to determine the most eligible student. In the event no such determination can be made, all eligible students shall be deemed valedictorians and awarded this distinction with honors.

This led to heated arguments over the nature of a full academic review of a student's records, with faculty members arguing such wording included a review of the student's middle school and, should it be necessary, elementary school years. Parents responded that "on the basis of academic performance during the years of secondary education" explicitly limited such a review to the high school years. The debate had started a year before I was hired, and five years later, the school board had simply given up trying to reason with the unreasonable.

Hence, nine speeches.

They were good speeches, though. The first reminisced about the transition from middle school to high school and speculated on the transition from high school to whatever came next. The second discussed athletic achievements. I drowsed through that one, but only because in four years, I'd been to one competition and that was because I made a wrong turn on my way to the local ice cream shop. The third expounded for fourteen minutes on the joys of being in the school band and the sorrow of losing our beloved band director. The fourth and fifth speeches worked in tandem to deliver a very detailed list of seventy-eight milestone events that had occurred during the past four years. A roar of applause, catcalls, and air horns stalled the fifth when she mentioned the death of Osama Bin Laden. The sixth gave a humorous recounting of the class' favorite teachers, complete with several none-too-subtle barbs aimed at me and Mrs. Hyde. All of my Composition students laughed heartily when mention was made of the student who refused to speak directly to me for a week after I refused to give her an extra credit point due to a spelling error. The seventh thanked the administration and faculty for all their hard work and mentoring over the years and the eighth thanked the parents for their support. The ninth speech was the *pièce de résistance*, however, a soaring and eloquent statement of everything the Class of 2012 really felt distilled into a single sentence: "But, in the end, there's only one thing that really matters: we're finally outta here!" It was spoken with such a smirk that everyone other than the graduates forgot to applaud.

Principal Hunter then asked the graduates to stand. Mrs. Hyde and I moved to the podium as the first row of graduates filed toward the side of the dais. We had agreed at practice earlier that week that the first half would be my responsibility. Aside from making sure I didn't rush one graduate on stage before the previous graduate was off, my task consisted solely of correctly pronouncing everyone's name.

"Bradley. Taylor. Allen."

He ascended the stairs, shook hands with the board, and accepted his diploma to a smattering of applause.

"Anastasia. Theresa. Antesia."

More applause.

"Zachary. Benjamin. Anton."

Hours passed.

"Beverly. Jolene. Bernard."

More hours passed.

"Tobias. Oolong. Gong."

Bodies crowded in the hallway outside of the gym following the ceremony. Gowns unbound fell to the floor or found themselves stuck in crevices in the walls. Everywhere, camera flashes illuminated paired and triplet smiling faces. Brothers and sisters, fathers and mothers, boyfriends and girlfriends, best friends, casual acquaintances, lovers, distant relations, teammates, mentors, employers, and ministers all hugged and cried and offered advice and remarked on the too rapid passage of time.

The faculty congregated at one end of the hallway. Occasionally, one of us was led away by a grateful student for a photograph or handshake or farewell thanks. Most of us stifled our yawns and kept the checking of our watches to an absolute minimum. Miss Connors chatted gaily with Mr. Young, the chair of the science department, alternating between looking enthralled and looking exasperated. Mr. Young's wife had left him for a twenty-year-old tennis pro at the start of the spring semester. He'd apparently moved on from wallowing to hitting on women better than half his age. The fiend. I held no claim to sainthood, but at least I kept my deviant behavior outside of the building. Mr. Young was trying to get laid at a high school graduation. The only people who should ever do that are the graduates.

Disapproving of his behavior, however, did not mean I cared enough to save her from whatever foul and depraved canoodling he had planned. But neither did I relish the idea of posing with false smiles for a group of children who only days earlier had told me they'd never take another English course because of the misery I had inflicted upon them. Typical teenagers being melodramatic. Neither *Moby-Dick* nor the past hundred years of literary theory is that bad.

Miss Connors excused herself and drifted toward me with the faux casualness of a woman who hopes no one notices she's in heat. I had only seconds to act so I weighed my options:

1. Run down the hall as fast as possible in the opposite direction. Effective, but probably excessive.
2. Glad-hand the nearby rednecks and offer them my own advice for the future. No. Most of them loathed me for my refusal to accept redneck slang as legitimate communication.
3. Jump into a deep and meaningful conversation with the math department. No. It's been scientifically proven math kills testosterone.
4. Explain "one-night stand" to Miss Connors and hope for the best. No. Reasoning with a woman is like explaining number theory to a dead beetle.
5. Pretend to be drunk. Not entirely plausible without the strong aroma of alcohol, but in the absence of an alternative...

Fortunately, Principal Hunter got to me first.

"Did you fall asleep up there?" she asked in a discretely low voice.

"Not that I recall." And I really couldn't, but that might have been because I had fallen asleep.

"You looked startled every time I looked over at you."

"Vertigo. I thought I was going to fall off the edge of the dais."

"Vertigo?"

"Yes, ma'am."

"The stage was only a foot and a half off the ground."

"It's terribly embarrassing."

"Right. I need to see you in my office before you go."

"I'm not doing anything right now."

"I need to see everyone out."

"So, what, five minutes?"

"Do you have plans or something?"

"As soon as I'm dismissed, I'm on vacation, so yeah, I have plans. They include getting absolutely wrecked and waking up tomorrow with a tattoo of two parrots mating on my ass."

"I'm so glad you feel comfortable enough to say things like that to me."

"Understand, the tattoo will be located on my ass. It won't be a rendering of my ass on which two parrots are mating."

Forty-five minutes later, I sat in a spinning chair in Principal Hunter's office and admired the pictures of her family. She had two sons, one an accountant in Houston and the other an electrician in Toronto. Both had married their high school sweethearts, and if the pictures were any indication, their wives had been beautiful during their formative years. The accountant had a single daughter, a chubby little monster who took after her mother. The electrician and his wife had no children, which I couldn't help but admire given their already advanced ages. Another few years and they'd have the fertility of a graveyard. Or maybe they didn't want children at all. Common people, the ones who find their careers and relationships unfulfilling, place an inordinate premium on parenthood, as if the act of procreation somehow verifies one's worth. They rob intercourse of all the fun to be had, instead focusing on an end result that may or may not happen. Those who find themselves incapable of traditional procreation spend obscene amounts of money in pursuit of that elusive offspring, again suffering in the name of the possibility of a John Doe, Jr. And those happy accidents? "Oh, we couldn't be happier that our little unplanned bundle of joy decided to take up every last second of our time for the next eighteen years." There are plenty of people who make fine parents, parents who truly want and love their children, people for whom children are an added bonus, but procreation is an instinct, a biological imperative. Let's all not take it so damned seriously.

And what about those who choose to defy their biology and refuse to reproduce? The species will yet survive, so why all the hostility? Isn't a child better off being born into a family that wants it, that can truly love it? Even those who choose sterilization to reduce their carbon footprint for the good of the planet are treated better than the man who admits he just doesn't want to be a father. If parents could see what a teacher sees on a daily basis, see the ways their children behave and hear the things their children say, maybe more people would opt out of this particular program.

Then again, the little bastards do become interesting once they can wipe their own asses and stop watching *SpongeBob SquarePants*.

Principal Hunter walked in, flipped off her heels, and stepped barefoot behind her desk. "So, Mr. Sane, your four years are over," she said as she eased into her chair.

"Is this going to be a serious conversation?" Because I'm way too sober for that.

"No, no, not at all. I just remembered at your post-evaluation conference, you asked me about the tenure process and whether you were in line for that and whatnot."

Shit. "What did I do?"

"You didn't do anything."

"So why are you firing me?"

She laughed in genuine surprise. "Julian, I have no intention of firing you. You've become a real asset this last year. I'd be crazy to let you go." She opened a drawer and removed two tumblers and a bottle of Dewars. "Care for a drink?"

Now it was my turn to be surprised. You expect that kind of thing to happen in advertising agencies, but not in a high school. "Sure." What else could I say?

She poured. "Now, if you did something like this, I would fire you." She handed me one of the tumblers and then raised her own. "*Salute.*"

"*Na zdrowie.*" I took a sip and then set the tumbler on a file folder near the edge of her desk. "So what exactly are we drinking to?"

"I always have a drink at the end of the year. Reminds me that at the

45

end of the day, I'm still alive."

"How's that?"

"Every now and then, a person has to do something for herself. Especially in this business."

"I agree." I took another sip. "I take it my tenure is—"

"You're right on track. Unless you somehow really screw up before the August board meeting, you're looking at a secure position here."

"That's good. Security is good." I'd never doubted the district would grant my tenure, but having it confirmed was still a relief. In those days, it wasn't uncommon for a teacher to make it to the end of his fourth year only to be summarily dismissed with vague references to cutbacks or job performance or a changing political climate. "Yeah, I'll drink to that." I took a larger swig and relished the burn at the back of my throat. It burned like victory.

Principal Hunter took a small sip. "So how's it been, these last four years? Everything you thought it'd be?"

"More or less."

"Which means no."

I had to laugh. Whatever else she might be, my boss was quick. "The kids are different from when I was their age."

"Oh?"

"I wouldn't have thought ten years could make that big of a difference."

"What kind of difference?"

"It's small things. Take their homework. When I was their age, everyone did their homework, even the bums. And if you didn't do your homework, you sat there with your head down and hoped the teacher didn't notice and embarrass you in front of the entire class. Now, the kids take a certain pride in not doing their work."

"We don't have the backing at home. Parents don't see education as a priority. At least, not around here."

"But when did that happen? When did we become the enemy? I may not have liked all of my teachers, but I didn't view any of them as something to fight against."

"These kids today… if they wanted to, they could do a lot of damage.

They could rise up and go on strike and there wouldn't be a damn thing we could do about it. God help us if they ever figure that out."

"They don't need no education."

"Exactly."

I drained the remainder of my tumbler. "Well, this has been fun, but I do have things to do."

"Big plans for the summer?" she asked as I rose.

"Not really. Catch up on my sleep. Work on my novel. Eat three square meals a day. Read *War and Peace*. That's probably it."

"What's your novel about?"

"A school shooting."

She laughed. "Okay. I suppose there's a market for that somewhere."

"I hope so."

"Well, have a good summer. Don't do anything you'll regret."

That thing about hindsight? Yeah, well…

Chapter 4
Sex and Candy

At dawn the morning, but first night.

A rush and then a warmth across the brain like millions of spiders. An assembly driven half mad with relief.

Let us drink to our despair! Let us drink to ourselves!

The shouting in tongues sacred and profane. The smack of wet glass against dry wood. The hysterics of shocked receptors. Lines across her stomach. Lines across the porcelain. What dreams will come from these lines like alabaster slugs? A faint glow trailing across the sky. A soft blur like feathers against the stars.

One for every life. Let us drink to those who have lived! Let us drink like men! Bless us, oh Lord, and these our drinks! Where is tomorrow? There is no tomorrow!

In vino veritas.

You do nothing! Your mother smells of rotten fruit! I fucked your wife! Fists through open air. Blood. Spittle. A growl to a howl.

Gentlemen! Gentlemen! This is a place of business!

A pause and a shake. Laughter through ethanol. A cheese sandwich. Blonde blue jeans.

I like the way you handled that. What can I handle for you?

Swaying against the rhythm of sonic noise. Pressed against the folds. Warm and wet. The taste of salt and copper. Release. The calm sleep of surrender.

And then she was sitting in a chair on the opposite side of the room from the bed. Only it wasn't exactly her. The her I could remember, in the cloudy haze of my hangover, had blonde hair and a much rounder face. This her had dark hair with no highlights, a fairly uncommon sight. She also had thick eyebrows, again in contrast to the prevailing fashion. Her skin wasn't pale but neither was it terribly tanned. Her lips had been painted a faint pink, her nails black, and her jawline was angular in a pleasing way. She was wearing some kind of running outfit and reading the latest issue of *Maxim*, apparently oblivious to my awakening.

"Normally, I'm not hung over in my dreams, but give me a minute and you can crawl—"

A sudden wave of nausea hit. I barely had time to lean over the edge of the bed before the contents of my stomach came up. For whatever reason, a trashcan had been strategically placed to catch the vomit.

I rolled back into bed and wiped my mouth.

"It's about time," Whoever-She-Was said.

Not trusting my stomach to behave, I gave her a weak thumbs-up. The room wasn't quite spinning, but it did have a discernible tilt to it, to say nothing of the awful taupe patina of the walls. I closed my eyes and raised my arms to my head, but the motion was too much and I vomited again. When I turned back, the woman in the chair was gone.

"Now you're hallucinating," I told myself. "Maybe let's not do that again."

I rolled onto my side and drew up my legs, attempting to cradle a stomach that was growing more sensitive by the minute.

"Do what again?"

I snapped upright and then groaned as my stomach knotted itself into a clenched fist the size of a HoneyBaked ham. The nausea returned and I leaned over my vomit bucket, but after a few moments, my stomach relaxed. I wiped my face and realized I had been sweating profusely. Heavy

49

drinking always makes me sweat like a pig. I tossed back the duvet and saw that I was wearing a pair of blue jeans but no shirt or socks.

"Sorry. I didn't mean to scare you."

My uninvited guest stood silhouetted in the bathroom doorway. She was taller than the average woman and slender enough that in the right clothing she'd look like an advertisement in *Vogue*.

"Nice to see you smiling instead of puking."

I eased my legs over the edge of the bed until I was sitting. "I didn't realize I was smiling."

"Yeah. Happy thoughts?"

"My own personal *Vogue* model is asking if I'm having happy thoughts. Tell you what: hop into bed and give me a few happy thoughts. I'll make sure you enjoy it."

She raised a brow. "Does that kind of thing actually work for you?"

"I'll tell you in a few hours." I gave the mattress two solid pats. "Hop in."

Admittedly, the previous evening had been a debauched affair and my mind probably was recoiling a bit from the unrelenting horror of the morning sun, but that was nothing when confronted with the sheer loathing that entered her face. Only once before, when I leaned in to kiss a woman at the end of a blind date, had I seen anything remotely resembling the level of disgust and recoil on her face. My date had raised her hands to ward off my advances and retreated backwards, asking, "What are you doing?" in a voice so distant I might have imagined it. Whoever-She-Was merely stood in the doorway, mouth agape, eyes wide, hands frozen in place.

"I'm guessing from your reaction that I'm not dreaming. You're actually here."

She nodded the slow nod of the truly terrified.

"Okay, well, that's embarrassing, but now I'm curious as to who you are and how you got into my house."

Her eyes darted from side to side and slid along the ground in search of an answer.

"Let's not stand on false modesty, please. You were just sitting in a chair in my house watching me vomit. I'd like an explanation."

She clenched her hands together. "Mr. Sane, you were about ready to pass out in the street last night. I wanted to get you inside so you'd at least be safe. You looked really, really bad, so I figured I'd stay and make sure you didn't die in your sleep."

"Well, thanks for that, but if you're not here to distract me from my hangover, you can leave."

She bent down and retrieved her purse from the floor. "Yeah, I think I should go now."

"Who the hell are you, anyway?"

For a moment, she looked slapped. Then she threw her purse with a force her slight frame belied. The blow shocked me, unexpected as it was, but my shock was nothing compared to her shock.

"Oh my god, I'm so sorry!" She was covering her mouth with her hands and looking as though she had just witnessed a Frenchman removing one of my testicles with a small fruit knife. "I didn't mean to do that! Are you all right?"

In a flash, she was beside me, a wet rag being dabbed at an almost imperceptible scratch. Normally, I would have taken advantage of her proximity, but this was not a normal situation. I still had no idea who she was or why she cared that I had almost passed out in a ditch somewhere. Strangers don't worry about other strangers, not in America, and even those few psychotics who do display a certain bent empathy for their fellow humans are not inclined to spend any longer than absolutely necessary tending to the most damning wounds.

She kept dabbing the rag at my head, moving slowly from one side to the other, stretching her body against and then across mine, her breasts pressing into my arm, her hair tickling my chest. Her face bare inches from mine. Our eyes perfectly aligned. The warm perfume of her breath. The faint glow of powder on her cheeks.

"I'm sorry," she was saying. "I mean, I know you have, what, two hundred students each year? Makes sense you wouldn't remember all of us."

Students? "What?"

"It's okay. I just overreacted, that's all. I thought you might have remembered me. Kinda girly to get upset over something like that. It'd probably be cause for concern if you did remember all your female students."

I was rapidly losing my moment. "I think I just had an aneurysm. You were what now?"

A series of sharp knocks at my front door interrupted us. I didn't want to move for fear of what might happen both to my stomach and to my last shreds of decency, but when a second series of knocks followed on the fading echoes of the first, I made up my mind to tell my visitor to fuck off and then deal with Whoever-She-Was. Maybe a brief intermission would give me time to sort things out.

At the door, however, freshly rearrived from some European shithole and recently tressed down, was my sister, who, luggage in hand and scowl on face, clearly meant to add to my morning troubles.

"It's about time, your excellency!" she shouted with that distinctly Sane combination of indignation and indifference.

"The hell did you do to your hair?" was the most neutral thing I could manage under the circumstances.

"You like it?" She turned to one side and then the other, mistaking my question for genuine interest. "It's all the rage over there."

"No, it's really not."

"You have to go to know, brother, and you haven't so you don't."

"Don't try that dramatics shit on me. It's too fucking early and I'm too fucking hungover."

But my sister was no longer looking at me. She was looking over my shoulder. In thirty years, my twin sister had not been surprised since glancing to the side of her plastic tub in the infant ward and realizing she had not been the only Sane born that day, but there she was, my sister the dramatist, speechless.

"I'm sorry," Whoever-She-Was said. "I, uh, I didn't realize you were expecting company. I'll, um, uh, get out of here now."

My sister shoved past me and, unbidden and undesired, entered my home. "No!" she said. "No. Nononononononono. Please, don't leave because of me. Julie didn't know I was coming."

"Julie?" Whoever-She-Was asked with a grin.

"It's a family thing. We're all pretty nuts."

"Yes, both of us are nuts," I said. "Thank you for—"

"Julie, don't be rude!" She stuck out a hand. "I'm Clara Sane. I'm Julie's sister. Obviously."

"It's nice to meet you, Miss Sane. I'm Lily. Lily Carter."

"Lily. That's a pretty name. And how old might you be, Lily?"

Lily gave a weak chuckle. "Oh, I'm, uh, nineteen. Eighteen. Nineteen in two months."

Oh thank god!

"Eighteen! Wow. That's a great age. I loved being eighteen."

Clara turned to me and mouthed "Eighteen!" with a glare intended to set ice sculptures on fire.

I shrugged. "Eighteen's great. It's great. Just great."

Clara turned back to Lily and began stroking her shoulders. "Well, you and I need to get to know each other. How about we go grab a... no, you can't drink. Julie, what do people get when they don't drink?"

"Coffee?"

"Yes! Yes, Lily! You and I need to get some coffee together this week."

"Um, okay." Lily looked at me with raised brows.

I shrugged. "That sounds terrific." I took Lily by the arm and pulled her to the door. "I think it's time to go. Thank you very much for... everything. You have a lovely day."

"You too, Mr. Sane. I hope you feel better."

Mr. Sane! "Thanks. Bye."

I shut the door and fell against it under the weight of my sister's sinister gaze.

"Julian, is there something you'd like to tell me?"

"I can't think of anything."

"Julian!"

"It's not what you think."

"You're not wearing a shirt! Or shoes or socks, for that matter! Hell, you're not even wearing a belt! In twenty years, I've never known you to wear jeans without a belt!"

"It's not what you think!"

"If I go into your bedroom and sniff your sheets, what am I going to find?"

"Okay, one, that's just creepy, and two, it's not what you think!"

"What is it, then?"

"I'm not entirely sure, but I know it's not what you think!"

"You're not sure! I come over to surprise my little brother and find him cavorting with a child of eighteen!"

"You're older than me by four and a half minutes and she's not a child. She's eighteen!"

"Ah! You admit it!"

"Admit what? Jesus Christ, are you listening to yourself?"

"Julian!" She threw up her hands and walked from the entryway to the living room, through to the kitchen, then back. "Swear on their graves."

"That is not cool."

"Swear it!"

Fine. "I swear on mom and dad's graves that I did not… I'm fairly certain I did not have sex with that woman."

"Julian!" Then she grabbed my hand and started sniffing my fingers.

"What are you—?"

"If you don't know, I'm going to find out!"

I jerked my hand away from her. "I didn't sleep with her! Christ! She was, I don't know, she found me almost passed out somewhere and brought me home. She was worried about me or something and that's why she stayed. Happy?"

"Why would I be happy, Julie?"

"Stop calling me that!"

"Do you have any idea how that looks? Do you get that you work in a town of 6000 people? Do you realize that she could have been one of your students? Probably was one of your students?"

… "There's nothing to suggest that she's one of my students."

"She's in Vespers. People don't come to Vespers for the waters. People are here because they were born here and will most likely die here. That's what happens in these small rural communities."

"What do you care? Isn't this exactly the kind of situation you'd put in one of your plays?"

"This isn't a play, Julian! This is your life! Careers end because of shit like this! You need to figure out who she is and then deal with her!"

"Clara, listen to me: I have a hangover and your constant berating is not helping. I did not have sex with her. I admit that I do try to fuck anything in a skirt. There is nothing else to do in this town. And I have done very well for myself. My headboard has more notches in it than the average slave had scars on his back. But I am not stupid. I would not fuck someone who could be one of my students."

She gave me a hard look and started chewing on her lower lip, a sure sign she was at least considering that I might be telling the truth.

"Sis, I am not that stupid. My dick is going to be the end of me, yes. We both know that. But I would never do that to a student."

She sighed. "I know, Julian. I know you wouldn't do anything like that intentionally."

But…

"But you've always been too close to your students."

"I get along with my kids. It makes my job easier and it makes learning a little more fun for them if we're all at ease with one another."

"Julian." She hugged me, tighter than I was entirely comfortable with, and rested her chin on my shoulder. "I worry about you, bro. You're all I have. I don't want anything to happen to you."

I gave myself over to her embrace. There is something to be said for a sibling's embrace. "Nothing's going to happen to me."

"Promise?" Her voice sounded muffled.

"Are you crying?"

"I'm trying to."

Clara Sane: tear-free since 2006.

My sister was right on at least one point: I needed to identify my mysterious guest and then decide whether to ensure she never returned or take advantage of her youthful interest in me. I started with a Facebook search, but her profile was private and all I could see was what I already knew: Lily Carter, Vespers, IL. Twitter proved equally useless, informing me only that a number of individuals I knew followed her, which, given a town of 6000, was hardly surprising. A basic search turned up nothing of note beyond links to a number of outdated social network profiles. I ran my hands through my hair and then spun myself around in my chair, stopping in full view of my bookshelf.

On the third shelf from the top, nestled between the complete works of Shakespeare and the *Nova Vulgata*, was my yearbook collection: the four *Effetes* from high school, the six *Warblers* from college, and the most recent three *Canons* from my time at VCHS. Good, old-fashioned physical books: still the best possible resource. It took less than a minute to locate her: Lily Carter, Class of 2011. Athletics: track and cross county. Extracurriculars: Drama Club, Speech Team, and Math Team. Voted "Best Smile," "Everyone's Friend," and "Most Likely to Cause World Peace." The photographs showed her with curled hair and an immense smile. Running, posing, or just leaning against walls, she gave off the unassuming intensity of the truly beautiful. Aside from the typical airbrush scrubbing all yearbook photographs receive, her photographs were remarkably naked. Only in her prom picture did she wear any makeup, and even then, it looked garish, like needlessly added decorative lines on a silver teapot. Her posturing was girlish, oftentimes distinctly immature. In one picture, she had crossed her eyes and was trying to touch the tip of her nose with her tongue. The look would have been patently absurd had her eyes not been laughing. In almost every picture, people surrounded her, boys who wanted to bask in her presence, girls who hoped some smattering of her would rub off on them. No matter how many bodies crammed into the frame, though, she stood alone, blurring the rest of the photograph so that she held dominion like an uncrowned queen.

I flipped through the pages, wondering who she was beyond the girl in the pictures. How could I have forgotten a girl like her? Girl. Woman. Girl. Student. Eighteen. Woman. Then it appeared, in the top right corner of page 102. The caption read simply, "Lily Carter and Mr. Sane look nervous together. What have they been plotting?" and there was something illicit to the picture. We stood side by side, our bodies slightly angled toward each other, comical looks of surprise on our faces. What were we plotting, indeed. My right hand was frozen in an open reach or retraction—I couldn't be sure which—and the level of my hand suggested whatever I had done or was about to do was highly inappropriate. Behind us, students crowded into the cafeteria for what appeared to be some kind of class meeting. Why would I have been in a meeting for the Class of 2011? Had it been a start-of-the-year meeting, I would have had my own class' to attend. But then, how many meetings are there in a year? How many times do large numbers of students gather to discuss issues about which only a fifth of those assembled care?

Regardless of the place, why had I been photographed with a student at all? The only other pictures of me were my faculty photograph and one of my announcing the king and queen candidates at that year's prom. She had called herself one of my students, implying she had not only been a student in the building but also in one of my classes. I wasn't working during her freshman year at all, and during her sophomore year, I was responsible for freshmen and juniors. For both her junior and senior years, I handled exclusively sophomores. By the time I began teaching seniors, she had already graduated. Perhaps she referred to herself as my student in the same way most students think of themselves, as students of the institution rather than of any specific individual. If each class averaged 100 students, that would have been at least 700 distinct faces over three years. No wonder I couldn't remember her.

Opposing the sheer number of students, though, was the woman herself. Any woman who looked like she did, any woman who elicited such a reaction, I would surely be able to remember. It wasn't simply that she was attractive. I'd known plenty of attractive women. Hers was that elusive sum effect that would cause otherwise reasonable men to wage wars or cut off digits if it meant spending a single night with her. She was something a man would spend countless monies trying to possess, even as he's aware he would never be able to keep her.

Why did I care? She was gone and I had no reason to believe she was

57

coming back. After all, it was chance she happened by at the exact moment I came stumbling down the road. So what if I couldn't remember her? I didn't need to.

But I wanted her. I wanted her, and nothing else mattered at that moment.

"How long are you going to sit there and look ponderous?" Clara asked from the doorway.

"Ponderous means—"

"I know what it means. I was playing with my words."

"Please don't butcher the English language. The plebs already have that well in hand."

"It's what we dramatists do. More importantly, I have something you might want."

"What's that, dear sister?"

She held up a cell phone, one of those fancy smartphones that could post to Facebook and Twitter while downloading apps for calculating phases of the moon or finding true love. It was, in other words, a sleek and sexy piece of ass that gave it up at the push of a button.

"Do you have that game where you only get one life and need to jump across large chasms without plummeting to your death and when you die the game locks itself so you can't continue playing?" I liked the idea of a one-shot game. Reminded me of life.

"No."

"So why are you showing me your phone?"

"It's not my phone."

Well, shit.

The coffee shop where I waited seated thirteen, which explained the absurd name the owners had chosen: Thirteen Cups. Five tables with two chairs each dotted the perimeter of the room and a counter with three chairs hugged the western wall. Against the back wall was a second, smaller counter dedicated to ordering. Everything was painted a creamed coffee brown. When the shop first opened, it did a decent business, but within two months, the novelty wore off. The only people who still frequented it were flannel-wearing hipster-wannabes who found sitting on the floor with a five-dollar cup of black coffee life affirming. Personally, I was happy to have a quiet place to write without people I knew stopping by every two minutes to ask what I was working on and if I had finally gotten around to grading that essay I collected three months ago.

I waved at the waitress to bring a refill and then returned to the sketch in front of me:

The end of the twentieth century was the last point in American history when an aspiring novelist could make it with a winning smile and a kick-ass book. I know this because I didn't get around to publishing my novel until 2011, and between 9/11 and the collapse of the American Financial System™, I'd taken it in the ass so hard and so frequently that I doubted I'd ever be able to sit down without wincing. 9/11 ensured the general populous would only read things bearing no connection to the real world, things that avoided sadness. People felt burned and with good reason, although I've never known anyone who's known anyone who lived in New York at that time. The publishing industry was taken over by pubescent wizards and poorly researched theology. Everything became for the happy shiny people, whoever and wherever they were.

And then the economy collapsed, much to the surprise of the pimps, whores, and thieves in charge of the whole sorry mess. Joe Danger earned a buck-fifty in food stamps every two weeks, but he still qualified for a variable rate mortgage on a $350,000 home. Who knew that would send the country spiraling down the proverbial toilet to join the likes of Greece, the Sudan, and Myanmar? Regardless, disposable income dried up faster than Cleopatra's warm place after she learnt that first Roman she canoodled with was a grunt and not an actual kingmaker. This proved a bad thing, leading to the widespread appropriation of online piracy as a viable alternative to actual capitalism, which ironically exacerbated the problem. See, we all still wanted things we could do without; we just couldn't pay for any of it. The Internet, acting as the great democratizing force its parents had always claimed it would become, made it a snap for every asshole with a modem and a few hours to download the latest Rhianna album. Never mind that we were frequently disappointed with what we got. The fact was, we could, and so we did. QED. Artists continued to produce works people continued to download for free, and very little money changed hands, dragging out the recession through two presidencies, neither of which was intellectually capable of understanding the problem, let alone of doing anything about it.

On the upside, there was comparatively little pressure on artists to produce anything significant, a fact most took advantage of. Sure, McCarthy was still writing, but for every one of him, we had thirteen variations of Lady Gaga. Not that we disliked Gaga, but the situation led to a mistaken view of her importance, as if she were the second coming of Madonna or the Beatles. Perhaps it was the collective need for stability, to find something meaningful, anything, and lock it in as part of whatever culture we had left. Then again—and I can't be alone on this—if our cultural identity was to be inexorably linked to Lady Gaga, I'd just as soon be Greek.

What a load of crap. What had I said in 500 words?

The waitress set a fresh latte on the table. She tried to make small talk, a lonely girl trying to fill a quiet hour, but my failure made me irritable and I waved her away.

"How extravagant of you, casting away women like that!"

Lily stood with her back against the main counter. The waitress walked to the opposite side and took her order: a regular coffee, black. Lily paid, smiled, and indicated my table.

"I believe you have something that belongs to me," she said as she sat down.

I reached into my pocket and slid her cellphone across the table. For whatever reason, I felt like a drug dealer. "I would have called, but your home number wasn't listed."

"I don't have a landline. And thanks for rifling through my contact list."

"No, I—"

"I'm just messing with you. You are way too jumpy."

"Can you blame me?"

Her coffee arrived and we sat in an awkward silence, an amused smile tugging at the corners of her mouth. The waitress looked at each of us in turn and then stalked off with a look of co-mingled confusion and disgust.

"People seem to be getting the wrong idea about us," Lily said.

"I noticed. My sister warned me off you."

She laughed and tossed her hair. "She has a pretty name. Clara. Is it short for something?"

"Mom loved silent films. She thought Clara Bow was the epitome of that era, of the glamour and grandeur, or something like that. I've never really understood it."

"At least she's not named after a funeral flower. My mom worked in a flower shop in high school and loved the smell of lilies, so…" She shrugged. "Guess it's better than the alternative."

"Flower?"

She laughed. "How did you end up Julian?"

"Flavius Claudius Julianus. Dad loved antiquity. He saw Julian as a man walking backward while the world walked forward."

"Interesting. Your parents are—"

"They died. A few years ago."

"I'm sorry."

I shrugged. "Anyway, you have your phone back, so I'll be seeing you."

"Can I finish my coffee?" she asked as she raised the cup to her lips and peered over the rim from beneath lashes that seemed thicker than before.

"I think one of us needs to leave."

"But that would make me so sad," she said, adding in a low, underlined tone, "teach."

I saw her straddle me right then and run an eager hand down my pants.

I felt her tongue graze mine as I pushed up her t-shirt and cupped a breast in my hand and pinched her nipple erect. I felt her take hold of me and begin tightening then easing her grip with an urging rhythm.

I stood, hit my knee on the underside of the table and subsequently knocked my latte over. Lily grabbed a fistful of napkins and started cleaning the spill.

"Oh, crap!" Her tone changed almost instantly. What had been playful moments before became deeply earnest. "I'm sorry! I didn't mean to scare you! I was just... after what happened with your sister and all, I just thought I'd have a little fun with you. I'm sorry. I didn't mean to make you uncomfortable."

I rubbed my wounded knee. "I'm not uncomfortable."

"No, I know. I meant—"

"Lily, it's fine. I know what you meant. I need to get going." I thought for a moment. "I need to pack."

"Pack?"

"I'm going on vacation in a few days. I need to pack... you know. Pack." When bad things happen to good trains of thought.

"Where are you going?" she called as I opened the front door.

"The Caribbean."

Outside, I turned to glance through the window at her. She waved and mouthed, "Have a good trip!"

A liar succeeds only when the liar himself accepts his own lie. A vacation was an easy lie, an insignificant lie, but even then, I knew I was in trouble. I knew I was lying to myself, which would have been forgivable had I been lying to make myself happy. Everyone does that. But no, I was lying to keep myself from collapsing. It was a lie like a bullet, a bright, shining bullet of pure magnesium shot straight into my ribcage.

I might not have known anything else about her, but I knew I wanted her. I wanted to see her stripped and writhing against me in unbridled frenzy.

And I would.

Chapter 5
House of the Rising Sun

Infatuation is what happens when the mind tries and fails to rationalize the body's physical desires. In those first few days following our coffee shop encounter, I lusted after Lily Carter the way a man lusts for heat after wandering the Artic Circle for a week. I would be watching women walk down the street in their sundresses and the wind would twist their skirts about them and splash their hair into a torrent and I'd hear Lily laughing as she tried to control the mess. A woman in the supermarket would lose her balance and stumble into me and I'd feel Lily pressing her body against mine as she nursed my injured brow. I couldn't pass a flower stand without the mingling scents evoking her name. My skin itched like a junkie's. A knock on the front door or the honk of a car horn sent my pulse fibrillating. Even in dark bars as I preyed upon more age-appropriate specimens, I found myself searching the room for her face.

Desire, whether material or sexual, is an infinitely simple construct. A man desires to possess those things he does not already possess. Why he desires the things he does is irrelevant. It is enough that he desires them, desires ownership over more and more. Sexual desire is even simpler. The primal instinct to spread one's seed given a postmodern turn. The act being divorced of reason or purpose. The beatific honesty: to fuck is to fuck, not in answer to any biological imperative, but simply to act. How many conquests had I justified in that manner? But physical love is an act shared by two, and all of them shared in the act. They accepted our love as nothing more than what it appeared: two bodies conjoined for an hour or two. I knew enough in those days to know sex is not love anymore than a wedding is the marriage. Perhaps that is the greatest curse of my generation: the all-knowing reduction of the sacred.

There were other times, though, quieter times when my thoughts passed over her physical attractiveness and lingered on something less tangible, more obscure. It was this intangibility I found so frustrating, and the more I tried to focus on Lily's physicality, the more prominent the intangibility became. But if it wasn't merely her body I craved, what was it?

Clara's thoughts on the matter were limited and a trifle obsessive. "You cannot have sex with your student," she told me repeatedly.

Rationally, I knew well enough not to act on any kind of impulse with a student, current or former. Student-teacher relations have a way of ending careers with spectacular pyrotechnical displays. The district was still coping with the aftermath of the countywide Year of Bad Teachers eight years later. Parents looked back on those days as confirmation that educators had become too friendly, too close, too approachable.

2004 started with a literal bang in the back of a school bus during a field trip to St. Louis to see a production of *Othello*. The teacher in charge of the trip, Mr. Clayton Romaine, later claimed he was one man put in charge of forty-five students and begged the administration to explain how he was supposed to watch all forty-five all the time. He was officially reprimanded but received no tangible repercussions, which became the main point of contention amongst the townsfolk when word broke that a female student was seen fellating a male student during Mr. Romaine's class not six weeks later. His excuse was that he just didn't see anything, those damn kids being so crafty at hiding their indiscretions. At that point, the administration had no choice but to remove him from the classroom, placing him instead in an empty room for eight hours a day to finish out the year at full salary before pressuring him to resign his position.

While Mr. Romaine played Solitaire in Solitary, a female teacher from nearby Freedom Community High School was dismissed from her position after being caught with the school's varsity football coach *in flagrante delicto*. The coach was reprimanded but allowed to remain on staff, either due to tenure or his stamina. The teacher was also reprimanded and though she too was allowed to remain on staff, she tendered her resignation a week after her reprimand. The security camera footage was eventually leaked onto the Internet and can still be found if one knows the correct filename for which to search.

More heinously, that March saw the secretary of Monroe High School lose her job after her three-year relationship with one of the senior girls was discovered. While cleaning the secretary's desk area, a janitor found an extremely graphic letter written by the senior to the secretary in a trash bin. When confronted with the letter, the senior broke down and admitted she had never thought of herself as a lesbian nor had any lesbian experiences prior to being told she was a lesbian by the school secretary. The secretary was fired and now works as a real estate agent. The senior went on to publish a memoir of those three years entitled *Naughty Bits*, which met with high critical acclaim for its sexual frankness but sold poorly.

In what might have been the most damning move a teacher could have made following such scandal, science teacher Helen Sheeley divorced her husband in early March immediately after his arrest for cocaine possession only to marry in June Charles Wollenberg, a 1998 graduate of Vespers Community High School. Mrs. Sheeley taught at VCHS for another six years before retiring at age 61.

So much in so short a time was more than the public could bear. The superintendents and school board members for Vespers District 1, Monroe School District, and Freedom Community School District 1 were ousted in August and replaced by groups of concerned parents and recently certified college graduates. Whether the situation actually improved or merely went deeper underground is anyone's guess, but the intervening years saw no further student-teacher scandals.

* * * *

Further complicating matters was the continuing presence of my sister. Clara's production of *Blasted* in a small theatre in Chicago had a number of watchdog groups hounding her with obscenity charges. During the scene in which Ian cannibalizes the dead baby, Clara deviated from the original script and added sounds of the baby crying immediately before being consumed. What I saw during rehearsals impressed me for adding horror to what was an already disturbing moment in the play. The critics saw it as leaping like a gazelle past any reasonable boundary of good taste. The production closed after only three performances and Clara hightailed it down south. She set up shop in my guestroom and began working on an original play, some morbid psychodrama about rape victims.

Clara has always been good company and great fun. She can drink most men under the table and knows more dirty jokes than most fraternity brothers. As a houseguest, however, she quickly situated herself at the center of everything. If I left the house, I had to tell her where I was going. If I shut myself in the study, she'd knock at the door to make sure I was okay. If I got up in the middle of the night with a bout of insomnia, she was up almost before I was out of bed.

"You haven't been sleeping, which means I haven't been sleeping, which means we need to deal with whatever is bothering you," she said one Sunday night or Monday morning.

"Nothing's bothering me," I said. "I get insomnia during the summer. I always have."

"Okay, so you're a little ADHD. With your job, that's not really surprising. Have a couple drinks before bedtime."

"Doesn't help."

She sat on the sofa's armrest and tugged at her nightshirt. "When's the last time you had sex?"

"Jesus, Clara!"

"What? That kind of thing can really mess with your head."

"I'm fine. Really. I get laid all the time."

In typically dramatic fashion, she fell backwards into the sofa cushions.

66

"God, I wish that was the same for me!"

"I really don't need to hear this."

"Do you know how long it's been since I've gotten any?"

"I'm not going to pry. This is highly inappropriate on any number of levels."

"Actually, I was high! And do you know how long ago that was?"

"Clara, really. Go to bed. Just... go. Don't say another word. Don't collect $200. Just go."

"Do you want to know what we did?"

"No. Please, God, no."

"Tell me what's bothering you."

"There's nothing bothering me!" I shouted.

Clara sat up and held her hands about ten inches apart. "His dick, I swear to God, had to be—"

"Jesus Christ, Clara!"

"C'mon, Julie! Talk to me! Let's dish! We used to dish all the time."

"Look. Nothing's wrong. Nothing's bothering me."

"He had this thing where he would twist just as—"

"Clara, it's nothing!"

"Ah!" She leapt from the sofa and stuck a finger in my face. "So there is something going on!"

"No, there's not! I just have something on my mind that I'm, you know, processing. I'm processing. I'm in my processing mode. Processing is not conducive to sleep."

"Okay, so is it a something or a someone?"

I started for my bedroom. "I'm going to bed. I'm tired now."

"So it is a someone. Julie's got a girlfriend."

"She's not my girlfriend!"

"Ah-ha!" Again with the finger. "You used to be so much better at this! In college, it would take eight or nine tequila shots before you'd fess up to anything. So, who is she?"

"She's no one. I'm not talking about this."

"You are talking about this. You want to talk about this." She waved her hand in front of her. "This is the conversation you want to have."

"There's nothing to tell. There's nothing going on. Really."

"Is she someone I know?"

"What?"

"That's a yes."

"No, you don't know her."

"Julian, you lie like Persian rug: flatly." She said it in an accent that might have been Middle Eastern but didn't really sound like anything.

"Clara, you've been saying that for twenty years and I still don't know what it's supposed to mean."

"It means I do know her and you don't want me to know who she is. Now why not?"

"Because it's not a thing. There's nothing. Like I keep saying."

"What are you hi—" Her smile dropped.

I swallowed. "I'm not hiding anything. I swear. Nothing is happening, nothing is going to happen."

She took a step forward and slapped me across the face as hard as she could.

"What the fuck?!" I screamed, cradling my cheek. "What was that for?!"

In reply, she slapped me again. And again. And again. Each time, harder than before.

"You son of a bitch!" she screamed.

"Don't talk about mom that way."

"How could you be so goddamn stupid?!"

"I think you're overreacting just a bit. Nothing has happened. She's been on my mind a bit. That's all."

"That's all? That's all?! You don't think that's bad enough?! You're not troubled by the fact that your first reaction wasn't to say, she is my student and this is wrong?!"

"I don't know what you want me to say. What will appease you at this point? Because, clearly, doing nothing wrong is not enough. Tell me, what will be enough to satisfy you?"

"Don't you dare! You don't get to be indignant!"

"What do I get to be, then?! You're screaming at me, slapping me, over nothing! I didn't do anything wrong! I don't know how else to say that!"

Whatever dam she had built up over the years finally broke, and her tears flowed freely. "Julian, I don't know what you think is going to happen between the two of you. I don't know if you want to date her or screw her or teach her or what, but I do know that no good will come of it. There is no way it will end well. It will end in tears! Yours. And hers. And mine. Don't do this."

"Clara, we've been over this. I am not going to do anything with a former student."

She wiped her eyes and sniffed. She shrugged. "Fine." Then she went into the guestroom and shut the door. In thirty years, there had never been a door shut between the two of us.

That morning, Clara gave no indication she even remembered our fight. Instead of dredging up further histrionics, she buzzed around the kitchen making scrambled eggs and fried potatoes. The Sane clan has always taken solace in food. I was in no mood for a second round, so I kept my mouth full, pausing only long enough to utter some trite compliment before stuffing my face again. After breakfast, we retreated to our respective rooms and let the silence fall firmly between us.

She was, in no uncertain terms, overreacting to the situation. Insofar as Clara felt it necessary to play the older sibling card, she was older by virtue of minutes, not years, giving her no substantive claim of superiority. Furthermore, her personal life frequently involved casual sex while on ecstasy or acid. I may have been a cad's cad, but at least I was reasonably sober most of the time. I could look a conquest in the eyes and know exactly who she was and what we were doing. The best Clara could hope for was to open her eyes and see the same guy she had been with five minutes earlier.

While our parents were still alive, several attempts at reigning in Clara's wilder tendencies were made. None were successful at doing anything other than causing Clara to temporarily cut off all communication with us. Following the accident, she seemed to run out of energy or interest, which suited me just fine, as I had no desire to fight battle after battle without backup.

This was different. Clara was, if nothing else, a fiercely rational and lucid individual who knew exactly what she was doing at all times and why. Her anger at our interventions, we knew, was merely a mask for some deeper despair that lurked beneath her actions. Her indignation at my involvement with a student suggested she firmly believed something had already happened, but then why not confront me directly? Why the teasing and mind games before a sudden blast of white-hot temper and then an indifferent, almost aloof morning? She was forcing confrontation, eliciting conflict for its own sake.

Let her rage, then, I decided. If she wanted a fight, I was more than happy to let her imagine whatever slights she fancied and try to make a target out of her kin, but I had no intention of playing along any further. All she needed was a few days to find something new to obsess over and she'd leave me alone, so I shut the door to my study, pulled out an old box from my graduate school days, and resumed my rainy day project: analyzing the differences between the British and American editions of John Fowles' *A Maggot*.

It was the kind of project only a literature buff could appreciate: going line by line through two editions of the novel, noting every single variance, and then speculating on the reasoning behind the variances. Admittedly, the conjoining of two sentences into one, as an example, is utterly insignificant to anyone other than a fellow writer. Stylistic choices at a mechanical level may be interesting, but they seldom shed new light on old words. Far more interesting—to the academic in me, at least—were the missing paragraphs and rewritten final sentence of the prologue. In the British edition, those missing paragraphs elaborate on a specific facet of the novel not introduced until the reader is significantly into the main movement, establishing a connection between the novel's murky origins and its final resolution. I seized on this during my last year at university, when such obsessions are not uncommon, reasoning rather naively that such an omission indicated further omissions. My thesis soon took precedence and the project was relegated to the bottom of a cardboard box, to be restarted only sporadically over the next several years. Never did I devote time enough to get beyond the first few pages in either edition. Had I, I probably would have laughed at myself and given up the project entirely. For all its folly, though, it served as a useful distraction. Besides, were I to ever actually finish my line-by-line analysis, I would hold the distinction of having read the novel twice at the same time.

As almost always happened, I quickly lost myself in the author's words and found myself reading for the text itself, relishing the plodding descriptions of the travelers' journey and the philosophical musings of the enigmatic Mr. Bartholomew. This in turn led me to revisit other of Fowles' writings: the first chapter of *Daniel Martin*, the final paragraph of *The Magus*, Miranda's last few diary entries in *The Collector*. I added to the extant marginalia in each book, a few faint scribblings in praise of word choice or pacing or depth.

It was well after dark when Clara knocked at the study door. I shut *Mantissa* and tossed it onto the nearest shelf, then unlocked the door.

On the other side, Clara held up index and middle fingers in a sign of peace. "Did you want to eat?" she asked. "I cooked. I went to the store earlier since you don't seem to keep any food in the house."

And just like that, we were fine again. Her inquiry, asking me to eat rather than simply placing food before me, coupled with a playful jab resolved the tension between us with a single mea culpa. She even smiled, not the harsh, guilt-ridden smile of a penitent, but the true smile that can only be shared between twin siblings.

I was hungry, and Clara had gone all out: a Caesar salad with homemade dressing and freshly grated parmesan, tomato soup with rice, Weiner schnitzel fried in lard—not butter, but real lard!—pierogi stuffed with sauerkraut, sliced Jewish rye bread, and a poppy seed roll for dessert. We both ate well and left little for freezing.

Later, we sat on my porch steps smoking a pair of decent cigars and sharing a bottle of very fine Scotch. I have in my bar at all times five single malts, each for a different situation: a twelve-year-old Glenlivet—my everyday drink, suitable for sipping in the evening while watching James

Bond films or European cinema—a ten-year-old Macallan aged in American oak casks—suitable when entertaining guests of either gender—a twelve-year-old Macallan aged in Spanish oak casks—suitable for sipping with male company over cards—a ten-year-old Laphroaig—suitable for sipping prior to public events—and a sixteen-year-old Lagavulin—the very finest of Scotches, suitable for celebration and lamentation, as well as gaining closure. Many are those who have argued the virtues of blended Scotch whisky, but those men, it must be noted, are missing at least one of their testicles.

Clara, a rare specimen of womanhood, could appreciate the finer liquors in life. She took appropriately small sips, gave the Scotch time to expand on her tongue, swallowed, and then breathed deeply. She also, in contrast with the overwhelming majority of her gender, could sit for extended periods of time in silence. The tension having been resolved, Clara understood one of the most basic truths of mankind: we will move on whenever possible.

But I didn't tell her of the dreams I'd had while dozing in between chapters. I didn't tell her of my kissing the length of Lily's naked and honey-glazed body. I didn't tell her of my teasing out her inner wet with my tongue. I didn't describe the look of pained ecstasy that crossed Lily's face when I twisted her hair in my hand and pulled at the moment of her climax.

What would I have said?

Chapter 6
Playground Love

10:00 PM. 6925 kHz USB. Three pounds of a gavel, followed by "The Star-Spangled Banner" played on a toy piano, followed by the opening of Depeche Mode's "Never Let Me Down Again," ending immediately following the first drum hit.

Then the baritone voice: "Good evening, friends and lovers. This is Midnight coming to you live for the next, oh, one, two, three, four hours on *Pomegranate Radio*: pirate radio for the masses. I'd like to get things started tonight with one of my personal favorites. Actually, it's only a favorite because of a recurring dream in which I feel up Sofia Coppola in some run-down Parisian hotel. Ladies and gentlemen, boys and girls: 'Playground Love.'"

Pomegranate Radio was a staple of Friday nights in Vespers, a weekly program of varying length composed of music selected seemingly at random from some infinitely stocked playlist, the odd political commentary rooted in a non-specific ideology Democrats and Republicans alike feared, and news and gossip from the local water coolers. How Midnight stayed so well informed was less of a mystery than how he kept his identity secret, given the number of listeners within broadcast range. No rural community

73

keeps secrets from itself well. From the outside world, yes, but never from itself. Surely someone somewhere recognized his voice. A voice as deep as his is a distinguishing characteristic. In four years, though, I'd never met anyone who claimed to know him.

But the man had his fingers on the pulse of the town. It was Midnight who riled the locals during the Year of Bad Teachers, dropping suggestive hints about each incident weeks before concrete details surfaced from any other source. It was Midnight who exposed the financial difficulties and eventual failure of Vespers Savings and Loan. It was Midnight who drew attention to Reverend Gus Hart's extramarital affair with Susannah Odell. In each instance, the man made a nonchalant comment between songs and then moved on before most of his listeners could process what he had said.

Pomegranate Radio fulfilled the promise of the Internet by offering a truly democratic source of information. No one was safe from Midnight's newscasts, but neither was anyone targeted for political or religious reasons. A factory worker could be exposed right alongside an alderman. An affair was given as much import as fraud. Black or white, red or blue, Protestant or Catholic: Midnight didn't see the world in binaries. He didn't even see the world in labels. He saw the world as a series of events and gave each event a primacy independent of the rest. His only allegiance was to the information itself.

Midnight was, in the end, the best source of gossip and rumor in the county.

Outside, the last storm of the summer poured down like the urine of a vengeful deity. No one knew it at the time, but that summer was to be the hottest and driest on record for southern Illinois in seventy years. Clara lay on the floor, flipping through a fashion magazine and periodically chuckling at the advertisements. I was sprawled out on the sofa, reading through Clara's latest scenes and making comments in the margins. Every so often, she'd try to sneak a quick glance at me, to which I'd respond by looking over the tops of my glasses and frowning. She'd roll her eyes and go back to her magazine. Every writer wants to be read, and every writer wants his readers to respond to his work. The catch is that every writer also dreads the reader who, ignorant of or indifferent toward the time dedicated to the work, responds with nothing but criticism. Clara, like most writers, suffered from an almost crippling anxiety when it came to sharing her first drafts, but unlike the vast majority of writers, Clara was extraordinarily gifted. Beneath the more visceral aspects of her plays was a profound understanding of humanity's reaction to suffering. Never did truth become subservient to spectacle. Never did violence or vulgarity become the play.

The song ended. "Gotta love that song. So swanky, so sultry, so let's-get-down-and-make-love. And speaking of love, I've been getting reports that some of the lovely ladies at AerisCo have been pumping more than just oil, so if you're looking for a hand, you might head over during shift change with a couple Franklins and see what you can see. Ask for Melanie. Tell her Midnight sent you."

J. Frank Wilson's "Last Kiss" began to play. Clara lowered her magazine. "Factory girls moonlighting as prostitutes," she said. "There's a shocker."

I grunted and continued to read. The protagonist was menacing her attacker with a metal dildo when the lights flickered. The receiver sputtered, regained the signal, and the song began playing amidst a wash of fuzzy static. Clara went into her bedroom, returned with a candle and some matches, and set the candle on the mantle. I motioned to the row of flashlights on the dining room table, which she had passed on the way to and from her bedroom, but Clara shrugged and waved a dismissive hand at me.

I finished the scene, set the pages on the floor, and rolled onto my back with my hands behind my head.

"What did you think?" she asked after a prolonged silence.

"You'll have trouble staging it," I said.

"But was it any good?"

"Yes."

"Are you saying that because it really was good or because I'm your sister and you love me too much to hurt me?"

"We both know I've never been that nice."

"True." She picked up the pages and started shuffling through them in search of the few marks I had made. "I misspelled misogynist. That's funny."

"Also tangerine."

The static suddenly grew in intensity, drowning out the song. I rolled off the sofa, switched off the receiver, poured two fingers of Glenlivet, and stuck a flashlight in my pocket. Scotch and a light source: always prioritize during a storm. A burst of lightning illuminated the windows with white light. The static fluctuated. Thunder ripped through the sky and shook the house. The bottles on the bar trolley clinked together. The lights dimmed, brightened, then shut off entirely. Clara struck a match and lit the candle. Another bolt of lightning, followed by another roar of thunder.

Then a tapping, then a rapping, a rapping at the front door.

Standing on my porch, wearing a white sports bra and matching compression shorts, arms wrapped around herself, was Lily Carter.

"Lily."

She was shivering something fierce. "Hi, Mr. Sane."

"What are you doing here?"

She drew a finger beneath her nose and then sniffed. "Can I come in?"

"What?"

"Julian!" Clara shouted as she shoved me aside. She took Lily's arm and pulled her inside, kicking shut the door with her foot. She led Lily to the sofa, then ran to the bathroom.

Rain dripped from Lily's hair onto her shoulders and ran down her slender arms and her white chest until it was soaked up by her bra. The fabric had turned translucent in the rain and the cold made her nipples stare out from beneath the thin gauze. I set myself against the wall and called for Clara to bring a robe.

"Get her a drink!" she called back.

"I am not giving a teenager alcohol."

"Get the poor woman a fucking drink! She's freezing!"

I went with a start to the bar trolley and looked at the five bottles of Scotch and the assorted bottles of lesser alcohol. I turned to ask if there was something in particular she'd like, but she was pulling her wet hair together and over one shoulder, causing more rain to spill down her body.

I poured a finger of the ten-year-old MaClaran into a tumbler.

When I turned around, Clara had wrapped Lily in my bathrobe and was toweling her hair dry. The sight of Lily wearing something I normally wore naked caused my grip to loosen.

"Don't stand there!" Clara shouted.

I held the tumbler out in front of me and crossed the room like an eighth grader attending his first dance. When Lily took the tumbler, her fingers grazed mine and left faint trails of damp in their wake.

"What were you doing out in this weather?" Clara asked.

"Yeah, you should be home right now." Wearing much more clothing.

Lily drank down the Scotch in a single go. I coughed.

"My car wouldn't start," she said between shivers. "I like to jog through the park at night. I ran back to my car when it started raining but I couldn't get it started."

"Didn't you have a cell phone?" Clara asked.

"I left it at home," Lily said. "I started walking and this was the first house I knew."

"That doesn't seem at all safe," I said. They both looked at me. "Jogging at night. Pretty girl, jogging in the dark, all alone. That doesn't… seem… like a good idea."

"I'll make you some tea," Clara said, never taking her eyes off me. "Julie, will you help me?"

I followed my sister into the kitchen. She set the kettle on the stove, pulled down three mugs from the shelf, and began measuring out portions of loose-leaf green tea.

"Something wrong, sis?"

"Your playground love is in our living room," she said.

"I didn't invite her in. You did."

"Would you rather I had sent her back out into the great deluge?"

"If I'm going to be yelled at again, yes."

"Grow up, Julian."

I stuck my hands in my pockets and walked back to the living room. If Clara wanted to be bitchy, she could do it without me.

Lily, meanwhile, had found Clara's play and was reading through it with a growing series of creases on her face.

"Clara, did you want a second opinion on your play?"

She came in with a mug of tea in each hand. "Why?" When she saw Lily, she gave a high-pitched *EEEEP!* "It's not finished! You can't read a play until it's finished! I'm not finished with it!"

I crossed my arms. "I got to read it."

Lily ordered the pages and held them out. "I'm sorry. I just saw it sitting here and got curious." Clara took the pages with a huff. "It's really good, though. What I read, I mean."

Clara paused. "Oh?"

"Yeah. I really liked how the guy kept telling her to look at him during the rape, how it wasn't enough that he hurt her physically. He needed to make her act as a witness to her own abuse."

Clara opened her mouth to respond, closed it, opened, closed, then turned and tried responding to me, only to suffer the same dry mouth. I shrugged.

"Mr. Sane was really good," Lily added.

Clara raised a brow but said nothing.

"All that stuff about how to read *Moby-Dick* stuck with me, I guess," Lily said with a laugh.

The soft glow of the candlelight against her features made her look older, lent her the age of maturity rather than years. Her laughter, which under the harsh light of day would have seemed girlish, sharply accented her maturity. She was not a carefree wood nymph flitting through her life. She was a serious young woman who could laugh at moments of absurdity.

"Call me Julian," I heard myself say.

We played games of chess and *Monopoly* for the next several hours. Lily proved to be both a clever strategist and a fearsome negotiator. Clara and I found ourselves at her mercy more often than not. If one of us gained the upper hand, it was a fleeting triumph frequently arranged by Lily to her advantage. My only victory on the chessboard was a draw she offered after I captured her queen with a rook that had somehow escaped her attention.

In *Monopoly*, her strategy was to purchase property near the corners of the board and then sink as much as she could into houses and hotels. She was often nearly broke, but one roll of the dice would transfer all of Clara's funds—or all of my funds—to her and she would laugh with glee. It was a simple pleasure, playing games in the middle of the night while sharing stupid jokes, the kind of pleasure a man grows out of once the real world intrudes into his life. Lily was young enough to enjoy it without any kind of pretense, and Clara and I were quickly caught up in her exuberance.

Between games, Lily talked about life after high school, about the joys of employment and bills. She had taken a position at the perfume counter of a department store, selling old women unguents to cover up the stench of decay with gardenias. She also spoke about her string of failed relationships with boys masquerading as men who pushed themselves on her too quickly and too carelessly. I cringed at the thought of some inbred redneck trying to grope his way into her graces with a six-pack of Budweiser and Led Zeppelin on the stereo. How many conversations had I overheard before class involving a weekend's indiscretions in the back of a pickup truck? But Lily was far less aloof than most women her age. Whatever companionship she sought needed to be tempered with genuine intimacy, not a sweat-soaked rendezvous.

"So I take it you're not dating anyone now?" Clara asked.

"No," Lily said. "The last guy I went out with didn't really want to watch the movie and kept pestering me to leave early. I think he got the picture when I accidentally spilled my soda in his lap."

I couldn't help grinning like some kind of court jester. "Good for you."

She chuckled. "Yeah, that kind of thing sours a girl on dating, especially around here."

"I can imagine."

Clara yawned. "Well, I'm tired, so I'm going to bed. Lily, thank you so much for what you said earlier." She walked to her bedroom door, paused, and turned. "Don't stay up too late, kids." She was on the other side of the door before I could throw anything at her.

Lily began straightening the room, collecting mugs and pretzel bags, packing away chess pieces into their velvet-lined box, and sorting play money into piles by denomination. Outside, the rain continued to pour.

Failing to find something more impressive or appropriate, I said, "This was fun."

She looked up from the pile of fifties in her hands. "Yeah, it was. We should do it again sometime."

"You have no idea how big you scored with Clara tonight."

"Just with her?"

I didn't respond. We both looked down awkwardly, like a pair of teenagers who bump into each other at the store while shopping for condoms and tampons. She resumed sorting with a noticeable increase in speed. A single bill slipped from her hands and both of us moved to catch it. Our hands froze as we reached toward first the bill and then each other and the bill floated to the floor. Our eyes met and the air between us warmed. Atoms hung suspended, torn between gravity's inescapable attractions emanating from either direction. A song of innocence and experience. A moment of trepidation and desire. I moved my hand to caress the soft of her cheek, the warm, smooth skin lightly flushing.

A flash of lightning startled us from our reverie. I drew back and ran my hand through my hair. Lily looked at the gaming materials still scattered across the floor.

"I'm kinda tired," she said, avoiding eye contact. "Do you mind if I finish cleaning up tomorrow?"

I couldn't respond and she didn't wait. We had agreed earlier in the evening that she would take my bed and I'd take the sofa. Thankfully, Clara and I had done laundry that morning, so I didn't have to worry about the beautiful young woman twisting alone into soiled sheets.

"Lily," I said as she was closing the bedroom door. The door halted, but she made no reply. "I'm sorry."

The door remained still for several seconds, then closed very slowly.

She crawled into my arms and nestled her small body against mine. Her hair still smelled like raindrops and her skin felt like silk runners. I turned her face toward me and she faded, leaving me to clutch empty space.

* * * *

Clara leaned over the kitchen sink and blew smoke out the open window. In the sink were two plates, two coffee cups, two forks, and two knives.

"There's coffee and toast," she said without turning. "No more eggs."

I poured some coffee and then watched Clara take a long drag from her cigarette, grit her teeth, then give a long, slow blow. The smoke caught the morning sun and went from pale gray to bleached white before vanishing.

"I thought you quit," I said.

She tapped ash into the sink. "She's at the park."

"What?"

"She went to the park for her morning run. She said she's normally there for a few hours."

"So?"

She took another drag.

I grabbed my keys off the table and headed for the door. "Thanks."

"Make sure you really want this, Julie. You'll never forgive yourself if you hurt this one."

The park was a three-minute drive made shorter by the lack of any other drivers on the road. What I was doing was stupid, phenomenally so, and yet I found myself driving with the intensity of a man who's running late for a party being thrown in his honor. If I didn't catch her then, I never would, and the thought of Lily Carter being caught by some half-wit yokel only accelerated the convertible. Why was I chasing her? Who was she that I felt so drawn toward a very public career suicide? Was it her youth? Her silken skin and lineless face and fragile body? Her effervescence? The complete absence of the cynicism of adulthood? She seemed untouched by the real world, not naively so, but unburdened by the knowledge that one day she would die and the worry of what she would leave behind. If she gave such concerns any thought, it was abstractly, without consequence. Was that the attraction? Woman as philosophical simplicity? *Make sure you really want this.* Did I? And if I wasn't sure, was it fair to go after her?

Or was there even anything to pursue? Was the notion of the two of us dancing solely in my addled head? *She's at the park.* She wouldn't have said that if she didn't want me to follow her. Unless she simply said it to say it. And if she had merely said it, what would that make me if I showed up hat in hand? Another lecherous teacher abusing his position. Was the possibility worth the risk?

Relationships die most often from inaction, like plants left unwatered on a windowsill. All good intentions are meaningless if they remain nothing but intentions. The housewife who grows apart from her lawyer husband not because he doesn't love her but because he never says it. The high school couple who take it for granted that they are dating because the one asked the other out to a movie once. The heart answers no authority but itself. If I felt anything at all, even if it existed nowhere but in my own mind, I had to act. It was an imperative beaten out through the rhythm of my pulse. Maybe she would laugh at me, at the sad old man flirting with a child. Maybe her face would scrunch inwards in confusion. Maybe she would scream in horror and flee from me. Her reaction no longer mattered. Any kind of answer would be better than a lingering question mark. I had to act, because the heart answers no authority but itself.

When I arrived at the park, though, I realized I had no idea what I was actually going to say to her. Fifteen years of panty peelers had not prepared me for anything beyond base physicality.

Lily ran along the bike path that skirted the park, her body already glistening in the sunlight like flower petals covered in morning dew. She was coming up on the parking lot when I pulled in. She either didn't see me or didn't want to lose her rhythm because she ran right past the row of spaces where I parked. As someone who has difficulty running a hundred yards, to say nothing of a mile, I must admit, she had fantastic form. Her limbs pumped in perfect synchronization, her back straight, her shoulders squared. Her stride never faltered. Her muscles tightened and loosened exactly as needed. Her feet landed on the concrete with a roll that seemed completely effortless.

She passed me twice more, the first time staring straight ahead but also curling the corners of her lips into a slight smile, the second time turning to look at me with a grin of girlish delight to which I responded with a grin of boyish delight. When she finally came to a stop, she went to her car and pulled a towel and a water bottle out of the backseat and began wiping her face. Her breathing went from heavy to normal by the time her face was dry.

"Hi, Julian," she said.

"Hello."

"How's it going?"

"Fine. How are you?"

"Hot."

"Yeah. You look really good." Err. "I mean, running." I waved my hand at something, though I'm not sure either one of us could tell exactly what I was waving at. "You look really good running. You know, good form. Really good form. Yeah."

She laughed. "Did you need something?"

"No. My sister mentioned you were here and I thought I, you know, should..." Should what, Sane? Does she even want you here? "You know."

"Is everything all right?"

Well, damn. "I'm sorry. Actually, I just came down here to apologize for last night. That was not at all appropriate for me to—"

"You wanna go for a run?"

"What?"

"Would you like to go for a run with me?"

I looked down at my cargo shorts and Pink Floyd t-shirt. "I'm an old man. I think I'd just be holding you back."

She started jogging backwards along the path. "Tell you what: if you can catch me, you can finish your thought from last night."

"I'm an old man, Lily."

She was getting farther away from me. "Okay. If it's not worth it to you, don't."

She turned and took off at full sprint, and after a moment of foolish hesitation, I took off after her.

Chapter 7
Video Games

I failed to catch her that first day, just as I failed to catch her during subsequent runs. The frustration of being so close to her, of experiencing her radiant body heat as she warmed up beside me for each run, became almost overwhelming. Only the ecstasy of watching the lithe movements of her body, the light bounce of her breasts, the tense-and-release of her thighs, kept me from losing the tenuous hold I maintained. Any other woman I would have taken hold of and pressed my lips to hers, my body to hers, but Lily was not to be won by force, by aggression. Her laughter and carefree girlishness called our courtship out for what it was, what all courtships truly are: a game with two winners. You will have me, her body said, but only when I have you. It was maddening. The smell of her sweat became the smell of her desire, and at the end of each run, she would turn her head to reveal a sly half-smile beneath eyes that dared.

Did I dare? The danger of such a public display provided a lukewarm shower, but even the threat of discovery seemed absurdly easy to rationalize away. We were, after all, doing nothing wrong. She was of legal age and I was no longer in a position of authority above her. An ethically gray area, to be sure, but one in which the facts were clear. The slight difference in our ages and the nature of our original relationship were no more than topics of awkward conversation. Still, canoodling with her in a public park would have led to questions neither of us was prepared to answer. As it was, our daily runs were grounds enough for the gossip mill to begin turning. Undoubtedly, whenever little old ladies with small dogs and nothing to do with their days gathered in groups of three or four, the topic of that curious schoolteacher and his student running in the park came up. They had nothing to do but speculate, though, which made such gossip's inevitability easy to ignore.

Besides, the image of an old man huffing after a young girl while trying not to pass out must have provided enough amusement to halt any serious concern. Here was a man who could barely make it around the park during the first few runs without dehydrating himself to the point of seeing blackness creeping at the edge of his vision. At the end of the first run, I sat down hard on the concrete and spent the next ten minutes trying to calm down, my stomach knotted so tightly water made me nauseous and my pulse racing so fast I felt certain I was going to have a stroke. She slowed down after that, never enough to let me catch her but enough to allow my body to condition itself to the exercise. On the second and third days I was sore all over, but by the fourth day, my legs were getting used to the exertion and I no longer felt like vomiting when I stopped. I focused on the woman running from me, on the prize awaiting me at the end of the race, and the more I focused on her, the less strenuous everything became. I didn't exactly enjoy the runs, but I became more willing—and more able—to participate in them.

She teased me mercilessly, whether intentionally or otherwise, and I let her, because every smile and every smile moved me just a bit faster and a bit harder toward my goal. Our goal.

A tacit understanding emerged between the two of us acknowledging our need to one day move beyond the confines of the park, lest the chastity of our relationship become its undoing. Lily began stopping by the house unannounced, not with any clear regularity but frequently enough for any neighbors who were paying attention to notice. We cooked for each other and played chess and watched old movies. Lily even took to acting out scenes from Clara's play so Clara could see what worked and what didn't. Lily was actually quite gifted as an actress, though she never expressed any wish to pursue it. We listened to records and danced in the living room. We read poetry aloud while sprawled on the floor of the study. Lily tickled the ivories while I blew hot air through a shakuhachi, and we laughed at our dissonance. We were at our best when we let ourselves go, when we forgot the differences between us and played at being a normal pair of kids dancing toward each other.

The biggest surprise was not the ease with which we fell into our courtship, but rather the ease with which Lily could manipulate me. Prior to her, I had no difficulty in manipulating women for my own pleasures. Cad that I was, I had refined my seduction technique into an almost automatic process: offer a disinterested ear and a quiet tongue before revealing the softer side of the pillow. Even the most complicated women fell, and the few who resisted provided a certain insight that proved invaluable in further refinement. Lily, by contrast, maintained a constant control over our relationship. It was at her behest that we remained so chaste. Even the most innocent of touches—a hand on the back, a stroke of the cheek— was met with a gentle-but-definite denial. It was also at her behest that each rendezvous—such as they were—remained limited to the park or my house. When I inquired about meeting at her house, she gave one of her half-smiles.

"A girl's gotta have some secrets," she said.

For whatever reason, this bothered me. Lily had her secrets and I never pried, but so lacking was this aspect of our intimacy that friendship was quickly becoming the only reasonable label. Though I volunteered very little about myself, she coaxed out bits and pieces with a startling frequency. She already knew from school that I was Catholic, but she uncovered my intense disdain for the Church and for organized religion in general.

"Religion keeps simple people from having to face reality," I told her one night over plates of spaghetti with homemade marinara.

If she took offense at this, her face gave nothing away. Nor did she offer the slightest response when I confessed to having conservative tendencies despite being a registered Democrat. My sister would have broken a bottle over my head, equating as she did all conservatives with Mussolini, Stalin, and Hitler. Lily merely nodded and said, "That's interesting," before moving onto a new topic altogether.

The longer we talked and the more varied our topics became, the less convinced I became that she was trying to get to know me. Her abrupt movement from topic to topic suggested a woman searching for something specific without knowing exactly what she was seeking. Was I some kind of bizarre enigma in her eyes? Were her coy and suggestive glances a means of maintaining control while analyzing? If so, her dedication was perverse, and I couldn't bring myself to accept her advances and retreats as anything other than the natural skittishness that accompanies something new and unexplored.

In this way, Lily managed to suggest a staged virginity, a purity for show rather than out of innocence. Her handling indicated more than a passing familiarity with men, and her reticence in discussing the details of her own life acknowledged a siren's most powerful weapon: mystery.

One morning, as we sat on a bench sipping water from the same bottle, Lily turned and asked, "So when are you actually going to catch me?"

She said it with such seriousness that I found it difficult to respond. "When are you going to let me catch you?" I finally asked.

Lily pushed up from the bench and started jogging backwards. "What makes you think I want you to catch me?" She turned and ran.

Clara enjoyed having another woman around, and whatever animus she harbored toward my latest obsession, she was nothing but cordial to Lily. The two of them lunched together and went for afternoon tea almost to the point where Clara saw more of Lily than I did. Lily's presence smoothed the rougher edges of Clara's generally good-natured teasing, though the two of them made for a frightfully caustic wit at times. Left alone, they gossiped and giggled like two errant schoolgirls, and more than once I heard my name mentioned from behind closed doors.

"So what are you guys doing tonight?" Clara asked after dinner one night.

"Julie's going to be lamenting all the things we could be doing but aren't," Lily said with a smirk.

"It's okay," Clara said. "It happens to every guy. After all the wear and tear, I'm surprised Julie's able to function at all."

"Oh my!" Lily gasped in feigned horror. "Is that a problem, too?" she asked me. "If so, I'm really not sure this will work out."

These more explicit teasings illustrated the only substantive issue to arise. To put it bluntly, I felt blocked. I had grown accustomed, as would any successful cad, to a certain regularity of release, a regularity that Lily's playful denial interrupted. I've never been a man governed by my genitals, but being so abruptly cut off from one's pleasures tends to have a negative physiological effect. In my case, friction burns caused by excessive stimulation.

Like most people at that time, I had a drawer where I kept my secrets hidden away from direct sunlight. This drawer was the bottom compartment of a wooden filing cabinet once belonging to my father. My secrets were the poems, plays, short stories, character sketches, drafts of novels started but never completed, carbon copies of love letters, literary analyses, outlines, course notes, reading responses, and translations collected over a period of fifteen years, all neatly organized by year, then genre, then specific date, then, if applicable, draft number. Most of the material ranged from the barely tolerable—any number of amateurish student poems lacking shape or rhythm, a sketch of two angelfish debating the aesthetic merits of *Hamlet* prior to being eaten by an anemone—to the downright embarrassing—chapters from *The Roadkill Ranger: A True Account of Three Nights in Lincoln*, a letter posted anonymously to Cordelia Wharton during the ninth grade in which I confessed my desire "to worship in perpetuity at the temple of your most magnificent femininity and bathe in the fount of your exquisite splendor." My course notes were quite often indecipherable—from Ancient Philosophy: "Atoms are eternal, invisible bits of being – no non-physical reality – non-being is real;" from Drama and Trauma: "inferiority complex; control; investigation only makes him feel worse; he can never gain the authority he wants; tries to perform in a role to gain authority; usurps former lover"—and the notes that weren't completely obfuscated bordered on criminally banal—from Methods of English Studies: "How is EIU funded? 120 million (total budget); 39.1% tuition, 73.33% appropriations, 17.5% dorm revenue, 16.67% grants."

Thus was it with some irritation that I stepped out of the shower to find Lily sitting crossed-legged on the floor of my study with my papers scattered about her.

"What are you doing?" I asked from the bathroom doorway.

"Reading," Lily said.

"Reading. Reading what?"

"Well, they all have Julian Sane typed on them, so I'm guessing they're the collected works of Kierkegaard."

"Funny. I meant, why are you going through my things?"

"Clara said you were in the shower but I could wait in here and that I might find something interesting to read."

"Did she? Clara!"

Loud rap music pulsing through the walls quickly followed the slamming of Clara's door.

"I love my sister, I truly do. Otherwise, I would have very little reason not to strangle her."

"So you wrote all of this but never showed it to anyone?" Lily asked.

"Professors read the essays and a handful of the poems were submitted to EIU's literary journal, but other than that, no."

"Did you ever try to get anything published?"

"Pick something."

Lily raised a brow.

"Pick something. Anything."

She looked at the heap surrounding her and chose a small stack of papers fastened with a single paperclip.

"What's it called?"

"'The Iguana Walks.'"

"It's about a college student who gets lost in a female dorm and uses the time he spends searching for a way out to muse about the differences between men and women. I wrote that when I was eighteen."

"So what's wrong with it?"

"It's eight double-spaced pages. What do you say about men and women in two thousand words?"

"Okay, so it's rough. You were eighteen."

"I had no business trying to say anything since I didn't have anything to say."

She found another. "What about this? 'In Praise of Editions.'"

"A man builds a house entirely out of the novels he reads. He finishes a stack of books and uses them to add new wings. I wrote that when I was in graduate school, so I was probably twenty-two. It was an exercise, an idea that I fell in love with but could never do anything with."

"I like it."

"You're also a child who hasn't formally studied literature the way I have. It's a cutesy little piece that does nothing, says nothing."

"Why does everything have to say something?"

"Because otherwise it's a waste of the reader's time."

"So waste some of their time. Some readers want that."

"The people who read *Harry Potter* and *Twilight* want that. The people who read Danielle Steele and John Grisham and Stephen King want that. No one will give a damn about any of that crap a hundred years from now."

"So?"

"So if I'm going to publish something, I want it to be a work I'll be remembered for. I want to still be read and discussed by serious people in a hundred years."

"You'll be dead. What will it matter to you?"

I shrugged. "It matters."

"Shakespeare didn't write to say anything. He wrote for the masses, and he's pretty well remembered."

"I'm not Shakespeare. I'm not even one of the King's Men. I'm just an average man with an average life who will never be read or remembered."

"Not if you never publish anything."

"I figured out a long time ago that I have no voice. Without a voice, even if I find something to say, I won't be able to say it."

"You're thirty years old and you've given up?"

"We lie to children all the time when we tell them they can be anything they want when they grow up. Not everyone has the requisite intelligence to be an astronaut, but we continue leading children to believe if they eat all their vegetables and drink their milk, they'll grow up big and strong and blast off to the stars. It's insulting and dishonest."

"You are so full of it. What happened?"

"I looked at my body of work and determined it wasn't worth pursuing."

"Everything I read was pretty good. Granted, I am an ill-educated slob from the wrong side of the tracks, so my opinion doesn't matter."

"You're too nice to pull off cagey convincingly."

"Then don't whine."

"I'm sorry?"

"You should be."

"I meant—"

"You're upset that you weren't the world's greatest writer at age twenty. Who is?"

"My point is that I have no innate talent and therefore will never be great."

"You're being too hard on yourself. Like I said, some of what you wrote was rough—very rough—but none of it was bad. I've read enough bad books to know what bad writing looks like. Yours is not bad writing. It needs refinement, yes, but it is not bad."

"Yes, well, we'll just have to agree to disagree on that."

She lifted a solitary piece of paper from the heap. "Who was Marty?"

"I have no idea."

She stood and held the piece of paper out in front of me. "If you had no talent, you wouldn't have written this. Whoever he was, he meant a lot to you, and whatever happened hurt."

I crossed my arms. "I'm not sure you are qualified to make such observations, however trite they may be, nor am I particularly pleased with having my personal life dissected by someone with whom I've been playing sexual cat-and-mouse for the past few weeks. Maybe you should grow up and stay the hell out of my personal things."

"Excuse me?"

"No, I don't think I will. And I think you need to leave right now."

She watched me, almost as if she didn't really believe I wanted her gone, and then slowly turned and walked to the front door. She turned back, handed me the paper in her hands, and left without a word.

Clara watched from the kitchen with her arms crossed and a scowl on her face.

"Asshole," I heard her say.

That afternoon, Clara sent me a text from the guestroom: "You were wrong. Apologize."

"Seriously? Isn't this a bit childish?" I cried through the walls.

"Fuck you" was the text I received in reply.

I changed into the running shorts I had recently purchased, tied my tennis shoes, and went for a walk. I circled my block, then circled the surrounding two blocks, then the surrounding four blocks, then the surrounding six blocks. I stopped and chatted with neighbors and other people I knew from work or the arts council or Rotary. I watched a group of small children bicycle up and down a single block, shouting incoherent things in that childish way. I purchased watery lemonade from three siblings for a quarter. I ran from the edge of the park to the horse barn on the outskirts of town. I took Main Street east to Division, Division south to Water, Water east to Clay, Clay north to Main, Main west to Division, Division north to Number, and Number west to the hospital, at which point I wasn't entirely sure where I was in relation to my house.

It was a good walk. My pulse was fast but steady and I had no headache. I was sweaty but not winded. At no point did I feel close to keeling over on the sidewalk. Those runs with Lily had been good for sculpting my body into something resembling fitness. Even the slight flabbiness of my midriff was receding. I was never going to be movie star attractive, but she was slowly forcing me to sculpt my body into something more, something better, something appealing.

But as soon as my thoughts turned to Lily, my irritation returned. My irritation was reasonably justified. A man's work is his own and no one, especially not a frigid teenager, has the right to rifle through his work without his permission and then give commentary as though she is in some way enlightened. The audacity of speaking out of turn about something she knew nothing about. For one thing, most of what I had written was bad, talentless and inept. For another thing, what wasn't outright bad was personal, such as the "Marty" poem she had so brazenly waved in my face.

Martin Schott had been a professor of creative nonfiction during my graduate school days. Marty, as he was affectionately known by most of his students, despised being thought of as an academic, preferring bawdy jokes and casual discussions to lectures and intellectual masturbation. His journal articles focused heavily on an appreciation of art for its own sake, as opposed to the general trend in literature circles at that time of dissecting one tiny aspect of a work in terms of a political or social dimension not actually relevant to the work. His essays read more like humorous reviews than serious scholarly work. What his students appreciated was his joviality and his laughter. He would routinely read excerpts from whatever we were studying in his Marty Voice, a voice that took nothing seriously and succeeded in accenting the words in such a way that the hidden absurdities came to the surface with a genuine glee. We enjoyed how unassuming he was, how he never pretended to be above anyone else simply because he had a doctorate. In a profession littered with pretentious douchebags who argued the phallic symbolism of the samurai sword in *Pulp Fiction*, he was an average Joe who liked Belvedere vodka, Hedy Lamarr films, and baseball.

What none of us knew, what I didn't discover until almost a year later, was that Marty had some kind of brain tumor. I sometimes wonder if the Marty I so idolized was real or if he was the byproduct of a brain waging war on itself. The other professors swore he had been an upbeat bastard for as long as they had known him, but he wasn't even tenured when he kicked off so what were their observations worth?

One day in late March, he didn't show up for class. We sat around for thirty minutes before the department chair came to dismiss us. Marty wasn't answering his phone, the chair said. Three of us drove downtown with him to Marty's apartment. The door was unlocked and Marty was slumped in an easy chair facing the television. A rerun of *Wheel of Fortune* was playing. On the floor beside him were several empty medicine bottles and an empty fifth of Belvedere. He didn't look sad or upset or angry. He didn't look like anything. He didn't even look like Marty anymore.

Lily, of course, knew none of this, nor had she asked, which gave her no right to infer any kind of closeness between Marty and myself. To violate a man's privacy and then draw conclusions based upon half a page of scribbled lines. Marty was important to me. He represented the kind of professor I one day wanted to be. Sure, I enjoyed intellectual masturbation as much as the next scholar, but I also wanted my students to view me as a human being, not some mythic white-haired Professor living in a tower shoddily constructed out of ivory, wood paste, and academic essays read by three other people. I was hurt and I was angry and so I wrote a cathartic little poem of no great merit. I never intended to publish it. I never intended for it to be read by anyone other than the grad students who were in his class at the time. It was how we coped with a shitty situation.

It was, more to the point, none of her business. Whether she did it out of base feline curiosity or a desire to deepen our intimacy, she had no right to invade my privacy.

My shirt was dark with sweat and in my legs I felt a pleasant burning. I sat down on a bench, wiped the back of my hand across my forehead, then stretched out my arm and grasped the back of the bench. It was an unusual gesture for me. I sit with my arms crossed or my hands on my thighs, sometimes with a fist tucked beneath my chin, but rarely do I stretch out an arm unless said arm is going around someone, and even then, I don't particularly relish the thought of being physically close to another human being in a sitting position.

Across the street, a murder of crows landed in an undeveloped lot and began pecking in the grass like soldiers poorly outfitted for jungle warfare. A car drove past and honked its horn and all flew away save for two. These two perched themselves upon an electrical wire and cocked their heads at each other. Birds stand unharmed on electrical wires because they stand in a single spot, never completing a circuit. Had those two birds touched each other, they would have fallen to the ground dead before they had time to realize their error.

Alfonso's was known for its twelve-egg omelets, omelets so large and so crammed a reasonable person could only eat a quarter of one before feeling gorged. Most of Vespers could eat better than half. Clara and I split one and still couldn't eat more than three-eighths of it. We pushed the leftovers aside and leaned back, Clara with a pen at her lips and a notebook open before her, me with a copy of Borges' *Ficciones*. Periodically, Clara would spring to life and hurriedly scribble ten or so lines before resuming her repose. Then she'd reread a section, groan, and draw lines through her lines.

"Mr. Sane?"

I looked up from my book to see a very tall man in a dark sport coat and gabardine trousers that didn't quite match the coat.

"Dr. Mengoweitz," I said, extending my hand.

"I don't mean to intrude. I saw you and thought I'd say good morning." He looked at Clara. "I don't believe we've been introduced."

Clara raised her eyes from the notebook to Mengoweitz's eyes.

"Dr. Mengoweitz, this is Clara."

"Hello, Clara."

"Hello," Clara said in as flat a tone as possible. No one interrupts Clara Sane when she's writing. No one.

"Girlfriend?"

"Eww," Clara said.

"Ah, no, sorry. Clara Sane. My sister."

"Ah! I see the resemblance now."

Mengoweitz laughed a politician's laugh. I tried to join, but Clara continued to glare at him while wrapping her fingers into a blood red fist around her pen.

"Clara, this is Dr. Alastair Mengoweitz, the president of the school board."

She looked at me, minutely raised her brow, then offered her hand. "Nice to meet you, Mr. Mengoweitz."

"Doctor Mengoweitz," he corrected. "And very nice to meet you, Miss Sane."

"So how is everything, Dr. Mengoweitz?" I asked, knowing if I didn't make small talk, he'd make it for me. "Anything interesting on this month's board agenda?"

"Oh, same old, same old. Hirings and resignations. Requests for money the district does not have. Endless reports from each building. I swear, these meetings are altogether insufferable. Makes me wonder why I run."

"Hopefully, next month won't be so bad. I believe I'll be on the agenda."

"That's right. Your tenure vote. Nervous?"

"Not unless there's something I don't know."

Legally, the vote was an unnecessary formality. Tenure was automatically granted to a teacher at the end of business on the first day of his fifth year in a district. The school board's vote was a purely symbolic gesture, albeit a welcome one in a profession where decent employees are seldom recognized. A framed certificate and a letter of congratulations from the board was presented at the first school assembly of the year. Family members of the newly tenured were invited to attend, and the students always got a kick out of seeing their teachers break down in tears. Provided she stuck around through the end of the summer, Clara would be my only family there.

"Very good, very good," Mengoweitz said. "No, you have nothing to worry about. I've heard only positive things about your classroom performance. Of course, I imagine I wouldn't know any differently since I've never actually seen you in a classroom." He laughed his politician laugh again. "Well, I won't keep you from your breakfast. Miss Sane, it was lovely meeting you. Mr. Sane, best of luck with your vote, though I doubt you'll need it."

"Thank you, Dr. Mengoweitz. Enjoy your day."

He turned and joined his wife, Millicent, and their six children: Mary, 19, Matthew, 18, Mark, 17, Luke, 16, Peter, 15, and Paul, 14. Clara and I watched them leave the restaurant. The wife and kids piled into a faded blue Volkswagen Golf. Mengoweitz slid behind the wheel of a British racing green Aston Martin DBS Volante. Apparently, that's what being the head of a radiology group that services every hospital in a 150-mile radius gets a man.

"What a dick," Clara said.

"He's alright. I'm actually surprised he remembered my name. The first two years I was here, he called me Wayne."

"Yeah, well, he can call you whatever the hell he wants. He ever looks down my shirt again, I'll choke him with his own unraveled testicles."

"He's a Mormon. They don't do that kind of thing."

"Six kids. Yeah, he obviously never thinks about sex."

She went back to her drafting and I to my reading.

Fifteen minutes later, Clara emptied her coffee cup. "Brother?"

"Sister?"

"Do you think they fuck with the lights off?"

I looked over my glasses at her.

"I think they probably fuck with the lights off," she said.

"Clara, please." Then, in spite of myself, I began to laugh.

I called Lily after we got home. She didn't answer, which didn't surprise me, so I left a voice mail. I called again two hours later and left another voice mail. I called again an hour later. I didn't leave a third voice mail. Three voice mails seemed excessive.

Lily responded in person rather than via phone call or text, which interrupted my rehearsal. She stood on the porch with her arms crossed and wordlessly refused to come inside. The look on her face confirmed what man has known for thousands of years: no woman between the ages of eight and eighty can be reasoned with. I sighed. I swallowed.

"I do not share things about myself with other people. I am a very private man. I apologize for being short and taking out my neuroses on you."

"That's it?"

Damnit. "I had more but I can't remember it."

"You called me a child."

"I apologize for that, too. The rest of your apology—"

"And a slut."

"Excuse me?"

"You called me a slut."

"I did not call—"

"No, you're right. You called me someone with whom you are playing sexual cat-and-mouse. I'm just a child. I'm easily confused."

Don't engage her. Don't engage her, Sane. "You're twisting my words around. Can you just come inside and I'll give you the rest of my apology?"

"What did you mean by that? If you weren't calling me a slut, what did you mean?"

Sigh. "You're eighteen years old, Lily. You're eighteen and I'm thirty and I'm having some difficulty with that. I don't know what I can and cannot do here. I don't even know what we're doing. I know we're not dating, but we're also not playing grab-ass, so I don't know what we're doing, but I do know it's not enough."

The look on her face now indicated I'd gone way too far. "Okay. Okay." She was shaking and her eyes were puffy. "How about you help me out of my pants and you can have me right here on your patio! Will that be enough?"

The tears were flowing. Her words were quaky and her breath was shallow. I reached out to comfort her and she slapped me much harder than I would have expected from a woman of her size.

"You don't get to see me cry," she said. "You don't get to make me cry."

"Lily, I don't want to make you cry. I wasn't trying to say… Look, I like you. That's probably the stupidest thing I could say right now, but I really do like you. I want go out with you. I want to buy you dinner somewhere. And yes, I would like to touch you. I'd like to kiss you. I'm sorry if that offends you, but it's true. And I am very bad at this. I have no idea what I'm doing. I'm completely and totally lost. I don't do this. Most women, I go out with them, I sleep with them, and then I'm done with them. Do you understand? I don't see women more than once. I don't know how to do this. I'd like to do this, but I don't understand how it works. I'm sorry. That's just the way it is."

Lily gave a weak sniffle. "You're turning red."

"So are you."

"I've been crying. What's your excuse?"

"The woman I am not exactly dating got me all worked up."

"Don't people your age need to worry about their hearts?"

"You're a mean one, aren't you?"

She shrugged. "The world's a scary place. A kitty's gotta have claws."

She wiped her eyes and came inside, and I presented her with the rest of my apology: the writings I wasn't irrevocably embarrassed by, arranged on the dining room table by genre and year. Lily ran a finger over a pile or two, lifted the odd page to peer beneath, mouthed sentences here and there. She glanced at every single pile almost as if she didn't believe they were what I said they were, and then she stood there in silence with her arms wrapped around herself and her back toward me for a very long time.

Then she turned and threw her arms around my neck and kissed me for a very long time.

"Not that I'm complaining, but what was that for?" I asked when we broke for air.

In a voice that was barely a whisper, she answered, "For catching me."

She kissed me again. Her lips tasted like salt and cherry lip balm.

Chapter 8
Tonight, Tonight

Lily read everything on the table that night. If she'd already read it earlier in the week, she read it again anyhow. She read slowly, going over certain pages two and three times. She revisited stories and poems after reading others, nodding and smiling as if something made perfect sense only after making some obscure connection. At first, I tried to offer commentary, interesting—to me, anyway—anecdotes about when something was written or what my thinking had been behind a piece, but she repeatedly shushed me, so I gave up and sat in the corner sipping Scotch. She started mid-afternoon and didn't finish until well after dark, stopping only long enough to accept a bottle of water during hour four.

Whatever her fascination, I was fascinated by her fascination. Watching someone read one's work is vastly different from knowing someone in the room has read one's work. It's less abstract, more of a shared experience. The reader's emotional reaction to the author's words is viscerally real in the creases and smiles and frowns and narrowed eyes, in the absentminded stroking of the lower lip or the silent mouthing of phrases or sentences or whole paragraphs. My poems troubled her, my stories amused her, and my essays confounded her. She was a body reader: the less she understood a passage, the closer she moved her face to the page and the more frequently she mouthed along, in full knowledge that many explanations were written between the lines. She whispered every line of poetry and followed each line of fiction with her whole head. There were times when her breathing seemed to stop entirely and other times when her breath came in excited bursts. She gave everything the same attention, the same seriousness, weighing each page not on the value of its printed words but on the earnestness of its author.

So many moments—every moment!—I wanted to go to her, to take her face in my hands and draw her lips to mine and collapse into her in tears of gratitude, but her beauty rebuffed me. She took not me but my words, and my words became her and she became my words. I was neither living nor dead and I knew nothing. I had leaned forward to kiss the sea, and the sea had kissed me. Silent and desolate and empty. Where would I be deposited, upon what mythic shore neither heaven nor hell but beyond both? To die, to sleep as the bliss of someone else.

As she reached for the final sheet of paper, I rose and went into the kitchen to prepare water for tea. Lily walked in just as the water reached the appropriate near-boil. She placed a hand on either cheek and held my eyes with hers. For a time, she said nothing. Then, after a long exhale: "I love the way you write."

It was the single sexiest thing a woman had ever said to me.

"Thank you."

She pulled my face to hers without the unrestrained passion of our first kiss, but with no less intensity. I slipped an arm around her back and drew her body closer. Her hands moved to the back of my head and neck and her fingers laced through my hair. Her lips parted and our tongues met. Our bodies curved together against the countertop, the refrigerator, the stove. She sucked on my lower lip, nibbled at my chin and along my jaw. I ran my tongue along her earlobe. She shuddered and let escape a gasp of pleasure.

"I take it his apology worked."

Clara was leaning against the wall.

Lily gasped in surprise and shoved me away, her face bright red with a look of horror. Eighteen. Not embarrassment, but horror. Eighteen.

"Hello, Clara. What are you doing here?" I asked.

"I live here, Julie," Clara said.

"I'm sorry," Lily stammered. She brushed back her hair and kept looking around her in jerky movements. "I'm sorry. I should be going." She brushed past me and avoided Clara.

I caught her arm and held onto it long enough for her to turn in desperation and silently beg me to let her go. My fingers loosened and she hurried to the front door. She stopped and said, "I'm tired," then left.

I watched her walk down the street from the window. Her gait was stiff and she kept touching her face. Behind me, Clara came up and rested her chin on my shoulder.

"Well, that was mature," she said.

"She's eighteen years old. You scared the shit out of her."

"If being caught with her hand in your cookie jar scares the shit out of her, she should keep her hand out of your cookie jar."

"Fuck off, Clara!"

"Oh, for Christ sakes, there are some peas in the freezer. Those'll take care of your balls."

I stormed into the study and slammed the door. As if the situation wasn't awkward enough for the two of us, we now had to contend with my sister being an intrusive bitch. Whatever. I'd call Lily in the morning and make sure she was okay, apologize for Clara's behavior, and then maybe we'd actually go out on a real date. We had crossed enough of the bridge to realize there was no point in looking back. When certain events are set in motion, they have to play out to their ends, whatever those ends may be. I had a feeling Clara believed she was protecting us from ourselves, that if she could keep us frustrated long enough, we might not have to face what she saw as the inevitable tragic ending. What she didn't understand was that neither of us could stop even if we wanted to. Lily's touch, tentative as it might have been, was not casual. Her timidity was the timidity of any new lover, a halting search for that moment amongst moments when she would surrender herself to an explosion of diamonds against the sun.

* * * *

I made reservations at Angelo's, an Italian bistro tucked away between a tattoo parlor and a barbershop on the town square. The food was decent and the pricing was such that we were unlikely to encounter any students. If we did, I could always claim to have run into a former student and, being the decent fellow I am, decided to buy her a meal while catching up on old times. Even as I settled on this excuse, though, a dank corner of my frontal lobe started tingling. Who was going to buy that I of all people was willing to share a meal with a student? I was loath to even shake their hands in congratulations.

When I called Lily to formally ask her out on what would be our first official date—good god, how I sounded like a teenager!—my carefully laid plans fell into a bit of quicksand.

"Dinner sounds good," she said, "as long as it isn't some quaint, out-of-the-way Italian place with dim lighting where we most likely won't run into anyone either of us know."

… "No, of course not, I'd never make a reservation anywhere like that." I was, after all, dealing with someone better than a decade my junior. "Do you like wings?"

"I love wings!" she said, and I could almost hear her eyes and smile explode. "Baba Yaga's?"

"Sure." Why not? Messy, but messy can be fun. "I don't have a reservation, but I know most of the waitresses there, so we shouldn't have any problem getting a table."

"Can we play the trivia game?" I could almost see her bouncing up and down in her room, and I tried not envisioning her doing so in a black bra and panties.

"Sure." I like trivia. Plus, there's always the chance for side bets.

"Great! Pick me up in an hour?"

"Sure."

When I hung up, Clara poured herself a finger of Glenlivet and looked at me with a mild amusement. I asked her to cancel my reservation while I showered and shaved. She shook her head and continued to smile the

103

smile of one who's seen all of this happen before. I washed, conditioned, shaved with my premium shaving soap and straight razor, blow dried my hair, added a wax for definition, moisturized with an unscented and alcohol-free shaving balm, and applied a spritz of cologne to my neck and wrists. When I exited the bathroom, Clara stood in my bedroom sipping her Scotch and shaking her head.

"Do you want to say something, dear sister?"

She responded with a single chuckle and closed her eyes and sighed.

I picked out a nicer pair of jeans, a plain white shirt, and a khaki sport coat. The look wasn't dressy or casual and probably a little eccentric, but my students had come to expect that.

I paused.

My students. My student. Eighteen.

"Problem?" Clara asked.

My student. Eighteen. "Stray thought. It's nothing."

"It's not too late to cancel."

I rolled my eyes and shook my head. Clara smoothed the arms of my jacket and straightened the shoulders and then ruffled my hair.

"Girls like a man who's a little rough. Makes 'em go all gooey in their naughty bits. But remember: if you get lucky, be sure to use a condom. And don't neglect her needs."

Clara was definitely my sister.

The person who opened Lily's door was not Lily. It was a man, a tall, thin man with biceps that spoke of years of manual labor. He had a fantastic head of thick hair the same color as Lily's. His facial features were masculine variations of Lily's own: bigger, a little rougher, but with the same sharp exactitude. He stood in the doorway with one hand on the jamb and the other in the pocket of his jeans and gave me the once over only the father of a daughter can give.

He turned his head and called into the house. "Lily! Your date's here." He turned back to me and stared with the unwavering patience of a chopping block.

We stood there man to man.

I had the suspicion he thought I might cut my losses and flee if he kept silent, so I extended my hand and put on my best collegiate smile. "Good evening, sir. I'm Julian Sane. I'm here to pick up your daughter."

He removed his hand from his pocket slowly and for a brief moment I expected him to pull a gun on me, but he took my hand in his and squeezed firmly, shook a single up-down motion, and released. "Florian Carter."

"Pleased to meet you, sir."

His face relaxed. He smiled. "And cut out this sir crap. Call me Florian."

"Alright, Florian."

"People don't call you Julie, do they?"

"Only my sister."

"Family's one thing. Gotta let family have their way."

"Absolutely."

He nodded. "I'm glad you understand." He continued to nod. "Yeah, family is the most important thing there is." He stopped nodding and looked at me apologetically. "You know, I hate to do this, seeing as we're both men, but… family, you know."

"Okay."

"I don't mind that you're older than my daughter. I don't mind you were once my daughter's teacher. I will mind if you disrespect my daughter."

Your pupils are dilated. Would you like me to tell you the other physiological signs of arousal?

"I completely understand."

He looked ready to deliver more of his defensive father spiel, but Lily came up behind him and placed a hand on his shoulder. Together, they looked ridiculously uneven: her the vertically challenged daughter, him the vertically gifted father. But there was no mistaking their relation, either by their physical similarity or by the way they hugged each other. He stroked her hair and whispered in her ear.

Lily stepped outside and smiled and I felt ten years younger, ten years less experienced, ten years less mature. She was wearing a light gray sundress that clung to her slight frame. Her hair was pinned up off her neck. She wore little makeup and needed none to look ravishing. I held out an arm, which Lily took.

As we walked down the path to the car, we glanced back. Lily blew a kiss to her father and I politely waved.

"Have her back by ten," he called after us, and I almost missed a step.

The maître d' was one of my usual waitresses and seated us immediately at a table as far away from the louder sections as possible, which, given the size of the restaurant, wasn't very far away at all, but at least we could communicate without having to shout. The maître d' handed me the menus, stole a glance at Lily, and looked back at me and winked.

Our waitress was also one of my usuals. Lily's presence surprised her, but she recovered quickly and made several comments about how nice it was to see me out with company on such a beautiful evening. Lily pinched her lips together to keep from giggling.

When the waitress left to fetch our iced teas, Lily leaned across the table and asked, "So how many of them have you slept with?"

The question provoked an almost uncontrollable gag reflex. "I try not to sleep with women I might need something from."

"They're very friendly."

"I tip well."

"How well?" she asked with a slight smirk.

"Very well."

Our waitress brought our teas and took our order: a double order of boneless wings spun in a Caribbean jerk sauce, with fries, celery, and ranch dressing on the side.

"So how many women have you slept with?"

"I'm not sure how you kids play this game nowadays, but my generation has always considered this pillow talk and not first date talk."

"Oh, I'm sorry. So how about that local sports team?"

"They're doing amazing this year. I'm especially impressed with What's-His-Name. He's really been bringing his all."

"Hasn't he?"

I chuckled. "A gentleman never tells. What about you?"

She raised a shocked hand to her mouth. "A lady never discusses such things." She grinned. "Do you have any idea how bad your reputation was when I was still in school?"

"I had no idea you kids gave me any consideration in your downtime."

"There's not much else to do on a Saturday night but drink and gossip about our teachers."

"And what did you say about me?"

"That you go through women the way hunters go through ammunition."

"Colorful."

"Is it accurate?"

"Why are you so interested in my sex life?"

"I find it amusing that my teacher might actually be human."

"You know you were never actually my student."

"Maybe we'll try that later."

"My sister might find that hot, but I'm not so sure. Actually, I've been meaning to ask you something."

"Forty-two."

"Funny. In one of the yearbooks, there's a picture of you and me standing together during your senior year. For the life of me, I can't remember what we were doing when that picture was taken."

"You touched my butt."

"I'm sorry?"

"It was raining and the roof above the vending machines leaked. I slipped on a wet spot. You were coming out of the cafeteria and stopped to help me up. In doing so, you inadvertently touched my butt."

"Oops."

"Yeah, I kinda jumped. One of the yearbook photographers was walking by and thought it was a cute moment or something."

"Interesting."

"Yeah. You were trying to seduce me even before I graduated."

Oh god! "Please don't say that ever again."

"I was kidding."

"Still."

"Anyway. I remember Mrs. Kawolsky asking me why we looked so guilty when they were captioning it."

"What did you tell her?"

"I said your fly was open."

"Thanks."

"No problem."

"Can I ask you something personal?"

"As long as it isn't my bra size."

"I already know your bra size."

She looked genuinely shocked but amused.

"I have a bit of experience in that department. But no, I wanted to ask, why are you here?"

"At Baba Yaga's? Well, there's this much older man—"

"Hey!"

"And I'm convinced he's trying to seduce me. Don't tell anyone, though, because I think I kinda like it. Hint hint, wink wink, nudge nudge."

"Cute. I'm serious, though. No boyfriend? That surprises me."

"Well, why don't you have a girlfriend?"

"Because I have deep-seated intimacy issues."

"Me too."

"I'm a manwhore."

"I'm a slut."

"No, you're not. I don't find that funny."

"It's okay for you to be hard on yourself but not for me to poke a little fun at myself? That's a bit of a double standard, teach, and not a little insulting."

"I'm not sure anyone would buy you as a woman of low moral fiber."

"Slut."

"Don't say that."

"Really?" She seemed surprised.

"What?"

"When I got you home that night when you were totally wasted, you said a lot of things far more colorful than that."

"I'm a very bad person. That doesn't mean I like it."

Lily shook her head. "Anyway, I date guys, but I don't hit it off with many of them. Sometimes I think I do but they don't, and sometimes they think we've hit it off but we really didn't."

"You're young."

"And so many guys are pigs."

"Exactly. I know all about being a pig."

"Why do you do that?"

"What?"

"All this self-depreciating humor. Do you really think that poorly of yourself?"

"It's part of my charm."

"I'm not sure how charming I find it."

"That's sweet."

"And that's dismissive."

"Why does this bother you so much?"

"Because you're a nice guy. All the booze and all the women and all the vulgarity can't hide that. You are a nice guy."

"I'll take your word on that."

"You're a romantic in a cynical world, and there is no defense for that."

"How do you know I'm a romantic?"

"You let me read everything you valued. Everything you've written is infused with idealism, a longing for the world to be better than what it is and a profound sadness that it isn't any better than what it is. Not anger but sadness. That's being a romantic. Look at your dissertation: *Closer to God: Notes on an Aesthetic for the New Literature.*"

"I pilfered the first part from Nine Inch Nails. Not very romantic. And anyway, I never actually wrote a dissertation. I never started on my doctorate."

"And you don't see that as romantic? Compiling notes for something you weren't currently writing but might one day?"

"I intended to go on when I made those notes."

"And why didn't you?"

"I lost my drive."

"How?"

"Isn't this all a bit serious for a first date?"

"Would you rather talk about the weather?"

"A professor of mine agreed to sit on my thesis committee and then killed himself less than a week later."

That shut her up.

"I never really got over it. I barely made it through my thesis and there was no way I'd make it through another four years of school."

"So you got your teaching certificate instead."

"That was easy. Learning to teach takes no amount of intelligence. Look at the idiots universities keep churning out."

"Do you enjoy it?"

"Sometimes. I like being able to talk about literature all day and expose kids to ideas they don't get at home. I hate the politics, but there's always going to be politics."

"But you don't like children."

"I like children. I like teenagers. They can be interesting at times, the way they're desperately trying to understand their world. They keep screwing up, but every time they do, they try something else. I like that about them. It keeps me young and it gives me hope."

"Hope?"

"Yeah, hope. That things might turn out better. That I might not be a complete fool. That maybe something I care about affects one of them."

"So things did work out."

"I suppose."

Our wings came and spared us further embarrassment. Lily took a wing and bit into it. I speared one with my fork and carved, stopping with a piece centimeters from my mouth. Lily was staring at me.

"Yes?"

"You are really pretentious."

"Is that a problem?"

In response, she picked up another wing and thrust it at my mouth. "Bite," she ordered.

"I beg your pardon?"

"Bite."

I took a bite, feeling supremely foolish and a tad self-conscious. Lily giggled and bit into the remainder of the wing. What a sight we must have made! Two overdressed people of mismatched ages eating out of each other's hands and somehow finding a carefree humor in it.

We laughed and talked and made fools of ourselves for the rest of the night. Lily talked about her one semester at the local community college—she'd dropped out at the winter break due to financial difficulties. Her roommate was a foreign exchange student who spoke only the most rudimentary English and insisted on cooking things Lily couldn't identify but which succeeded in stinking up the entire floor.

"I got the flu right before Thanksgiving and when I started throwing up as she was cooking… I think she got the point finally," Lily said.

Her father was a welder who sold his portion of the business to his partner after suffering a back injury. Her mother was a tailor who divorced her father to shack up with a lawyer from downstate who kicked her out less than three months after they moved in together. Lily hadn't spoken to the woman since the divorce.

"I needed a mom and she didn't care, so I don't care about her. That's easier than crying yourself to sleep every night wondering what you could have done differently."

The boyfriend situation turned out less interesting than I expected. Her first real boyfriend was a pimply lad named Kevin whom she dated her freshman year. Their relationship ended after two months when her father caught young Kevin trying to slip a hand up her blouse. Evidently, her blouse being tucked into her pants defeated him. Her second real boyfriend, Neal, was starting center of the varsity basketball team. They broke up after four months when Lily realized all he really wanted was a chauffeur. Then came a long string of casual dates accompanied by the typical high school gossip.

"It wasn't like I was carrying on with every guy I met. I just had a date most Saturdays. But then someone started saying I was getting around and then everyone started saying it, so I just stopped. It wasn't like any of it was really that fun. Too much stress."

She liked math and history, wasn't crazy about English—"Sorry!"—and thought science was way too confusing the way it was being taught. If she finished college, she wanted to go into teaching, possibly kindergarten or grade school—"But not middle school! Those kids are insane!" She did express regret at not being able to take Composition with me.

"That reminds me," I said as our waitress refilled our tea and cleared away our plates. "Why did you say you read *Moby-Dick* with me?"

She smiled and toyed with her napkin. "You remember Jessica Knight?"

"Sure."

"You know how she always had her binder out on her desk whenever you were lecturing?"

I didn't but nodded anyway.

"Well, she told me you guys were reading it for class and I wanted to read it. As a joke, she said she'd record all of your lectures so I'd know what I was reading. It became a thing, and that's how I followed along. By the way, you really should stop telling so many dirty jokes in class."

"Wow, that's weird. You know, only about a quarter of my students actually read any of the book and only about five of them read the whole thing. Why would you do that to yourself?"

"It sounded like something I should read."

"Hell—" I cleared my throat and tried to play it off. "Heck, even our librarian doesn't see any value in it. When I mentioned we were reading it for class, she told me she wanted to give it a go, and now all she does is bit... moan and complain about how boring it is. I still don't think she's finished it."

"Well, I enjoyed it, and you explained it very well."

"Thank you."

She started to say something, closed her lips, took a sip of tea, and then shook her head. "Actually, that reminds me of something I wanted to ask you."

"Okay."

"What was your dissertation going to be about? I mean, your other academic stuff was kinda out there, but it was all complete, so I could understand most of it. You just had notes for your dissertation and they were... a little... you know."

"Incoherent?"

She nodded.

"It wasn't going to be anything monumental. At least in hindsight, I know it wasn't going to be. At the time, I was really excited by it. Basically, I spent six years studying the various branches of literary theory, at the end of which I became very dissatisfied with this approach to literature. I saw theory as a kind of Academia-sponsored bullshit—sorry—as a kind of crap that was reductionist and oftentimes flatly wrong. I kept going back to Chinua Achebe's lecture on *Heart of Darkness* where he berates Conrad for being a racist and writing a racist book. Is there racism in it? Yes, but that doesn't make it a racist book. Any time I'd say that, though, I'd get yelled at. I'm a white male; therefore, I can't possibly understand oppression. My dissertation was going to be a response to all that. I wanted to call for a return to a focus on aesthetics, on an appreciation for the beauty of the work as a whole. Rather than dissecting a work into tiny little pieces and looking through a microscope for something that may or may not be there, I wanted to analyze why we appreciate certain things as works of art. Why does this speak to its reader? Why does it move us? How does it move us?"

"Art for art's sake."

"Kinda, yeah. But I wanted to go a step further, and this is what really excited me. I wanted to call out theorists on what I saw as a major hypocrisy. Any number of movements—structuralism, post-structuralism, postmodernism—made the claim that anything could be read as a text. Anything. Films, naturally. Songs, sure. Street signs, even. Grocery lists. Desk assembly instructions. User manuals for digital cameras. Anything could be read as a text. The problem was, no one was actually willing to do it. I shouldn't say no one was willing, but very few academics were willing to go along with this. It more or less became the purview of highly experimental postmodern fiction. I wanted to change that. I saw it as a natural outgrowth of our culture. We don't value poetry as a culture anymore. We don't value literature of any kind. Times have changed, and we need to change with them. We don't value poetry, but we do value music. We don't value novels, but we do value film. Why not make a serious study of these things? Instead of blow-off classes in cinema appreciation, why not make a serious effort to understand and to quantify the aesthetics of these works? Photography! Instead of leaving these disparate fields segregated, I wanted to unite them and declare their value under a single framework. A new aesthetic theory for a new literature."

"That sounds pretty ambitious."

"It was. Maybe not as ambitious as I thought at the time, but it would have been an undertaking. I was going to use three works as my exemplars: Jimi Hendrix' cover of 'All Along the Watchtower,' Nine Inch Nails' *The Downward Spiral*, the whole album, and Nina Simone's 'Sinnerman.' I intended to use all three to illustrate my ideas. 'Sinnerman' was going to be my centerpiece."

"Why?"

"Because it's a rendition totally its own. It's not a cover and it's not a version of an extant song. It's a reflection that exists independent of its originating object. It's absolute, definitive. It supersedes any 'Sinnerman' that came before. It starts off as a finger-snapping, gospel-influenced dance number, catchy but nothing special, and then it restarts itself. The song actually breaks under the strain of trying to be more than it is, and so it begins again. It stops and then it starts, but this time with fervor, with an aggression and an urgency that's not really present or believable in the first three minutes. Simone stops singing and plunges the listener into this bridge that noodles along until the music becomes its theme. The song is no longer about something. It actually becomes redemption and damnation, salvation and condemnation. And that's the brilliance! Not simply that the song juxtaposes contrary ideas, but that it does so while creating a total unification. Every aspect of the song works in tandem. Everything is drawn together. Everything."

When I stopped, I realized my face felt hot and I was almost out of breath.

Lily leaned across the table. "Did you notice that?"

"I think I got a little overexcited."

"I've never seen anyone get that excited over anything. Are you sure you want to teach high school for the rest of your life?"

I leaned across the table and kissed her for as long as I could comfortably hold the position. Then I called for the check and paid and outside I pinned her against a stone pillar while our lips sucked at one another and our tongues tickled against each other and our hands sought out the curves and crevices and slopes of our bodies until we were both breathless and Lily had to gently push me away and every breath from her mouth came as a tremor, a little earthquake, *un petite mort.*

Chapter 9
Llorando

I tried the small box nestled amidst purple tissue paper within a larger box, then the small box within its bag inside a larger box, then the small box within its bag with the handles tied together with ribbon, then the small box simply tied with ribbon. This I did for an hour until the floor of my study was littered with crumpled tissue paper and ribbon cutlets. The box contained a silver necklace from Tiffany's and bore the name of the store, as did the original bag, and what woman doesn't squeal with a summer-at-the-beach glee upon seeing the Tiffany's name? Clara claimed to understand this and suggested any number of packaging variations meant to surprise and delight but which provided her with much amusement at my expense.

The necklace I purchased during a daytrip to Chicago with Clara. She needed to meet with a theatre manager to discuss the new play and I took the opportunity to wander Michigan Avenue in search of a birthday present for Lily. An iPod seemed too impersonal and a Burberry purse too intimate, chocolates too mundane and flowers too simplistic. I looked at leather portfolios—what, exactly, was she going to do with one of those?—and fancy raincoats—which would not clash at all with her flip flops or tennis shoes. A clerk at Bloomingdale's almost sold me on a pair of purple leather gloves and a matching pair of earmuffs, but I felt that was too much like something to give one's mother. Besides, with temperatures running in the upper nineties every day, the thoughtfulness of such a gift might have been missed. It was only on a whim, one of those silly, oft-dismissed quirks that yields exactly what you've been looking for, that I stepped into the jewelry store.

The lady behind the counter, a twenty-something with a pretty face and affected manners, kept pushing diamonds—"We're well known for our diamonds," "Don't you just love how these sparkle?"—but Tiffany diamonds three weeks after our first kiss seemed too much too soon. Frowning at the potential loss of a commission she clearly needed to finish cosmetology school, the saleswoman set out a number of necklaces with single jewel settings, at which I shook my head and reiterated my earlier request for something understated. With an increased frown, she began showing necklaces with single pendants: two interlocked rings that made me slightly uncomfortable, a pinwheel composed entirely of wire hearts, a shopping bag, a penguin, a Scotty dog, what appeared to be a psychedelic lollipop… They were closer in execution to what I wanted, but none of them suggested Lily to me. They were too cheeky or too gaudy or too cutesy. I repeated myself: understated, romantic but subtle. The saleswoman rested her hands on the glass case and drummed the fingers of her right hand, and there it was, directly beneath those fingers: a thin, silver chain with a heart-shaped pendant and a tiny key attached. I tapped at the glass and pointed and nodded and handed over my MasterCard. Ten minutes later, I was walking down Michigan Avenue with a sea-foam green bag in hand and a tremendous sense of accomplishment.

Now, however, as I sliced off yet another length of ribbon and tried another version of gift-wrapping the damned thing, I wondered if maybe I shouldn't have gotten her an iPod or at least something with a slightly larger box instead.

But what girl doesn't like Tiffany's?

Girl? Woman. Fuck.

Therein lay another, much more considerable, problem. My consort was what? An eighteen-year-old girl? A grown woman? Given the present was meant for her nineteenth birthday, this shouldn't have been any kind of issue, but at the same time she was attending her senior prom, I was nearing the end of my twenties. Eleven years. They call women who date much older men gold diggers. What do they call men who date much younger women? Lechers. Satyrs. Bounders. What would they call me? Or, rather, what would they call her? Me, I could handle country bumpkin assholes expressing their far-reaching ignorance and intolerance, but what would happen the first time someone close to her posted on Facebook that Lily was the whore sleeping with her teacher?

Sleeping with? Hardly. Three weeks after our first real date and we hadn't actually been to bed in anything less than school-appropriate outerwear. What difference would that make in the minds of the general public? Who was going to believe a known manwhore had not conquered his wide-eyed ingénue, that fantastic, acrobatic sex was not the very heart of our relationship? What would Lily say at the first rumor? Would she laugh and give a curt, dismissive wave? Would she collapse into tears? Would she take to whatever social media sites were at hand and launch a full-scale defense? Every time I stopped to wonder, I found myself suspecting her reaction would be a combination of all three, though what that meant was totally lost on me.

But as I settled on the box-in-bag-with-bow approach and tied my final ribbon, I knew it didn't matter. I was committed, to Lily and I and to whatever would come after.

I showered and shaved, brushed and flossed, pulled a cream suit with a peach shirt from the closet followed by a light gray suit with a white shirt followed by a black suit with a light blue shirt followed by a pair of dark jeans, a brown sport coat, and a white shirt, settled on the jeans and sport coat, and dressed.

Clara answered the door while I vacillated between a necktie, a bowtie, and an ascot. Moments later, she knocked at the bathroom door and whispered something in French I barely understood but was unquestionably obscene. Then the front door opened and shut as Clara left for a night on the town, a night she had promised me would leave the house empty save for a sibling and his lover.

I decided against a superfluous neck cloth, ran a hand over my face to check for stubble, smoothed the lapel of my sport coat, took a breath, turned off the lights, and stepped into the living room.

Lily stood in the center of the room wearing a slender dress of black lace laid atop a floral design that ended just above her knees. Her arms were bare except for a thin, silver bracelet on her right wrist. Her hair was pinned up off her neck in a mirror image of our first date. She was even wearing heels. She held a black handbag with both hands in front of her. I belatedly realized I had been expecting a girl playing dress-up to walk through my door, with the pieces perhaps correct but assembled haphazardly and with no understanding of the total effect. Lily was the most put-together woman I had ever seen. She was disarming, and I found myself having to focus on the placement of my feet as I crossed the room.

Lily made no movement but bit her lower lip and dropped her eyes the closer I came, and it was only when close enough to hold her that I saw the nervousness, the girlish uncertainty at her appearance. I might have laughed had I not shared the same ridiculous nervousness.

I leaned my mouth to her ear and whispered, "You look angelic. Happy birthday."

She beamed and giggled and I wrapped my arms round her waist and pulled her in for a kiss.

We moved to the dining room. I held out her chair and then lit the tapers from a single stick match. I looked over the label on the bottle of dry Chardonnay in suitably silly mimicry of a sommelier, then turned it for her perusal. She grinned, pretended to consider the year, then nodded with faux indifference. I poured just a taste into her glass. She swirled it, sipped it, swished it.

"This will do," she said in her snootiest accent, "but truly, you must find a bottle of the '85. A vastly superior year."

I bowed. "Of course, *mon petit ange.*"

Dinner was an Italian spinach salad with homemade parmesan and oregano croutons, followed by mostaccioli with roasted tomato and basil served alongside a crusty ciabatta—the only thing I did not cook myself, as Clara took delight in pointing out—San Pellegrino with the salad, a dry Chianti Classico with the main course, and tiramisu and coffee for dessert. We ate slowly and with enthusiastic conversation about Italian cooking and Lily's desire to tour Italy's culinary regions. She took issue with nothing, not even the slightly too *al dente* pasta, instead complimenting everything and leaving nothing but the plates to clear away.

After dessert, we took our coffee and sat on the sofa and talked about films and music and a book of Catholic theology her sister had sent for her birthday and a book on quantum mechanics Lily had read the previous month. I played selections from Wagner and Verdi and Tchaikovsky. Lily spoke of her admiration for *Swan Lake* and *Parsifal* and her passionate boredom when confronted with *The Nutcracker* or *Aida*. She lay in my arms and I stroked her smooth skin and breathed in the floral scent of her hair for what seemed like hours.

I waited until her muscles completely relaxed and she began to succumb to sleep's siren song before whispering again in her ear. "I might yet have something more for you, if you're not too tired, that is."

She turned her head and smiled and I almost forgot where it was I had hidden her gift. I leaned forward to kiss her hairline and then reached to the side of the sofa where I had hidden the small bag beneath two throw pillows. I presented the bag to Lily with a sudden bout of trepidation: should I have gone with the diamonds?

Lily took the bag with equal trepidation, every woman knowing the jeweler by its bag. Slowly, she drew the ribbon from the handles and removed tissue paper until she withdrew the square box with lace ribbon tied at the store by a professional. Upon opening it, she gasped almost inaudibly and reached a delicate finger to touch the pendant within. I should have definitely gone with the diamonds. But she removed the necklace and held it up between us, then smiled and offered it to me. I took it and she turned and I fastened it about her neck, letting my hands linger upon her skin before drifting along her shoulders and down her arms.

She reached a hand to touch the pendant where it hung just above the tops of her breasts, but I caught the hand and raised it to my lips and kissed her knuckles, the back of her hand, her wrist, her forearm as I spun her around to face me. The necklace hung perfectly around her neck and brought just the right amount of attention to her cleavage without being obscene.

"Thank you," she said before peppering me with light kisses.

We watched a purported love story set in the city of angels that turned out to be a surreal noir about Hollywood and the death of dreams, and though I enjoyed it on a technical level, it was anything but romantic and I suggested we turn it off when the protagonist and her lover made a 2AM run to a bizarre nightclub populated by a blue-haired woman and a Hispanic gentleman in a garish red suit. Lily whispered she didn't understand the scene in the nightclub and I replied that some things are not meant to be understood logically but obey their own kind of reason.

I suggested we find some old black-and-white movie to watch. She took my face in her hands, my cheeks in her warm palms, and pressed her lips to mine, gently at first, then with growing urgency, spreading my lips and teasing my tongue. Her body fit against mine, our curvatures perfectly aligned. Hands took hold at the back of my neck and head. Fingers clenched and nails bit lovingly. Our lips parted and one or both of us sighed, my face nuzzled against the clean, pink skin of her cheek. Her mouth and tongue moved along my jawline and down my neck. I shuddered and the gentle convulsions ran from my body to hers and drew forth a trembling that gave her pause. Her head fell back and her eyes squeezed shut and she let issue a staccato of breath like the first triumphal cry of life. I buried my hands in her hair, in that cascade of jet-black lilacs, and kissed a neck of alabaster and baby powder.

With a moan, she lowered her hands to my shoulders and pushed me away and stood. Her breathing came in tremulous spurts. She dropped her eyes, then reached behind her. The zipper of her dress released its hold and the dress eased off her shoulders before falling to her feet.

"Make love to me."

A black lace bra against creamy white skin. Nipples excited and reticent behind their veil. A hand against her cheek, her neck, her collar, her

121

shoulder. A finger beneath a thin strap. The unlocking of a metal clasp. Release. Exposure. A breath of heightened excitement. Ripples in the wake of touch.

"Make love to me. Please."

The first unbuttoning of a shirt. The tentative drawing of fingers down a naked chest. The fumbling with button and zipper.

"Please."

Hands upon hand, guiding from soft and supple to warm and moist.

"This is wrong."

"Please."

Intrusion. Violation.

Ecstasy.

Chapter 10
The Freshmen

In the gloom of early twilight, the wine and coffee woke me in Lily's arms. The delicate feel of her skin against mine held me captive as much as her embrace, but the pressure in my bladder won out and I withdrew from her arms and the tangle of sheets and walked naked to the bathroom. I shut the door but left the lights off for fear of disturbing Lily's repose. I urinated, flushed with the lid down, washed my hands, and then tiptoed back to the bedroom. A diffuse light crept in between the blinds. In the murk, the folds of the sheets became harsh and jagged, like rocky growths protruding from beneath desert sand. Lily slumbered with her lips parted and breathed so slowly and so softly that I momentarily feared she had expired at my side in the night. I pulled back the sheets and sat down on the edge of the mattress, but before I could swing my legs up, I noticed dark streaks maculate against the white of the sheets. I lifted them farther and saw the streaks continue, darkening. I lifted until I could make out two legs and then let them drop as I returned to the bathroom. I shut the door and switched on the vanity light and immediately saw the fading bite mark in my shoulder. Then I looked down.

How did I not notice?

Why didn't she tell me?

I put on a pot of coffee and stood in the kitchen dark. What else was there to do? Wake her and demand an explanation? Pretend nothing out of the ordinary had happened and pray she would do likewise? And what of the evidence streaked across my bed sheets? How was that going to wash out? It was one thing to take a woman to bed in worship of Bacchus but quite another to offer up a virgin sacrifice. Why didn't she tell me? The allure of bedding a virgin is the same allure that launched the moon race: a base desire to get there first, ahead of all other suitors, and to embed one's flag in soil unsullied by the footprints of countless others. But consider the archaic reverence for the bridal bed. Few are the men who expect to marry an immaculate bride. To taste what no other has tasted is by its very nature to violate, to corrupt, to destroy. In days of yore, this was celebrated, but what joy is there in the corruption of innocence? Why delight in besmirching? With what reckless abandon might a man tear apart his lover in the name of intimacy?

Yet, I couldn't be blamed. Infatuation and desire had conspired against me. Yes, the corruption was physically due to my presence, but what corruption had I actually visited upon her? What had I taken that she did not wish disposed of? What concern could I hold it if she held purity in so slight esteem? This was nothing more than a panic attack, a gag reflex, worry for nothing. If there were an issue, she would have mentioned it beforehand. Lily was not some high school drama queen. She was a grown woman capable of making her own choices and living with the consequences. The best thing to do, I felt, was return to bed and pretend nothing was amiss.

But the bloodstained sheets held me like the flashing lights of a railroad crossing. This was not blood spilled in sacred ritual. There was no redemption to be had, no returning of what had been taken. Smeared was evidence incontrovertible of the reality that a child ceases to be a child, that all within that is good and pure and innocent is eventually tainted by a brute force from without. Future lovers would throw their heads back and let fall their tongues in laughter, knowing they cannot take what is not there to be taken.

Lily stirred. I replaced the sheets and smoothed them around her, then went back to the kitchen. The coffeemaker's water delivery apparatus was clogged, though, and only a thimbleful of coffee had collected in the carafe, so I sat down on the sofa and waited for the sun to rise. The longer I sat, the antsier I became.

I went out onto the porch and sat on the lowest step. In the blue haze of the early morning twilight, little could be heard of the town. The easy rustle of dogwood leaves in the breeze. The low drone of electrical wires. The airy and spacious *whoosh* of the odd car rolling down an empty Main Street. There were people about, perhaps a great many of them, but in isolation, hidden in the damp blue of morning. They jogged their morning jogs, grateful for the fleeting respite from the summer's heat. They walked their dogs and collected their newspapers from their front lawns. They stood as kings and breathed deeply and pounded their chests in triumph of something none of them could articulate. Another morning, another day. And soon the sun would set the horizon on fire and cut a swath along Main Street, from the flower shop and the oil refinery and the graveyard to the chocolate factory and the gas station and the abandoned restaurant, bathing a little town in a little life. The copper detailing of the courthouse clock faces. The old-fashioned streetlamps with green paint shiny and slick. The red and blue lettering of the banner advertising the summer Wine and Cheese Festival suspended at the northeastern corner of the town square. The dilapidated buildings home to meth labs on the south side of town and the imposing monstrosities with columns and pink stone walkways on the north side. The apartment complex with the wrought iron railing poxed with rust along the second story. The yeasty smell of bread from the Amish bakery mingled with the sugary sweetness of the chocolate factory to blanket the town in delight as the air warmed in the coming dawn.

I sat until the first rays of light reflected in a burst off the metal roof of the house across the street. Then I went back inside and lay down atop the sheets beside Lily, my arm draped over her back, my head buried in her hair.

At 9:17, there was a knock at the door, and, thinking Clara had forgotten her keys, I went to answer it. It was, however, not my sister. It was, in fact, Stephanie Shoulders, a recent VCHS graduate who had spent the better part of the spring semester bitching about having to read *Moby-Dick*.

"If you're here to resume complaining about my teaching methods, please understand that I didn't sleep well last night and would like some quiet."

"Ashley Park's dead." She said it in a voice totally devoid of affect, the way someone might read off items on a grocery list.

"What?"

"I wasn't sure if anyone had told you yet. I know you two were pretty close."

Ashley reminded me of myself in high school—an idealized version, granted—but I never considered myself particularly close to him. He was tall and lanky and had a natural charm that came from his being clever and not knowing it. He was always a highly sensitive child and even the slightest intimation that he had erred was enough to put him in a sullen mood for a week or longer. He had a decent head on his shoulders, though, and a spirited sense of humor, which made his teenage mood swings much more bearable. That he was actually dead was unthinkable. This was a kid who was going to live to be ninety and still wear berets and ascots and sleep with women a quarter of his age.

"No one's told me anything. What happened?"

"It was an accident. He drove into a semi."

"What do you mean, he drove into a semi?"

"He—I don't know—he drifted into oncoming traffic and had a head-on collision with a semi."

"Why would he do that?"

"It was an accident. Eric's dad says there's no reason to think otherwise, even with everything else."

"What everything else?"

"Well, you heard his girlfriend was pregnant, right?"

I shook my head.

"Yeah, well, they found out right before graduation. She went a few weeks later and... you know. Her folks found out somehow and apparently things didn't go over too well with them."

"They blamed him."

"I guess. I don't really know what happened, but someone said she hung herself in her closet not long after."

"Oh."

"Yeah. Anyway, I just thought you should know. I would have called but you aren't listed."

"I don't understand. Ashley gets his girlfriend pregnant. She has an abortion, then hangs herself, maybe, and then he accidentally drives head-on into a semi?"

"Yeah."

"What the fuck?"

"Yeah. I'm sorry. I thought you should know. I—" Stephanie stopped, her mouth frozen at the beginning of whatever she was about to say, and leaned to her left. "Um." Her eyes widened.

I didn't have to look to know what she had seen, but I did anyway. I quietly belted out a hopeful prayer that Lily was not standing somewhere visible.

She was, but at least she was wearing a t-shirt and not standing there skyclad.

I turned back to Stephanie and tried to smile it off in a way that wasn't totally creepy. "Well, thank you very much for letting me know. If there's nothing else, I need to find a way to bring down Facebook and Twitter within the next two minutes."

"Holy fucking shit!" Stephanie suddenly shouted.

I shut and locked the door to avoid the rest of what I was certain would be a very awkward conversation. Lily giggled and ran up to me and threw her hands around my neck and kissed me. I was in no mood for a morning make-out session, but the more I tried to extricate myself from her arms, the more ferocious her assault became.

When it finally became clear to her that I did not want to play, she leaned her head against my chest and sighed. "People had to find out somehow. They were always going to find out."

"I would have rather they not find out by seeing you walking out of my bedroom in an oversized t-shirt. There is not going to be a single tweet or wall post that says 'OMG Mr. Sane is dating Lily Carter!' All of them are going to read 'Guess who's fucking Lily?!?!'"

She kissed my cheek. "Don't be crude."

"And don't be naïve."

Lily let go and took a step back. "What's wrong?"

"Nothing is wrong. It's been a long morning."

"Julian, you're trying to pick a fight with me over something we both knew would have to be dealt with sooner or later. No, this is not really how I envisioned it happening, but it's done. It's out there. Stephanie's texting everyone she knows and everyone they know and it's out. You knew that might happen. We both did. So why are you mad at me about this?"

"I'm not mad at you."

"Yes, you are! What's wrong?"

Well shit. Fine. "Why didn't you tell me?"

"Tell you what?"

"Think very carefully, Lily, and tell me if there was anything I should have known last night."

"What are you talking—" She paused, looked away, snorted. "Oh."

"Oh. Yes. Oh."

She shook her head and muttered something.

"I'm sorry?"

"I said, I didn't want to freak you out."

"You didn't want to freak me out?"

"I was—I don't know—I was scared, I guess."

"Scared? Of what?"

"I don't know! I wasn't sure what to say! Be gentle with me? It wasn't like you were bringing out the leather whips and ball gags. I didn't want to spoil the moment with an awkward conversation that wasn't going to matter."

"It would have mattered. It would have made a difference."

"How so?"

Reasoning with a woman is like teaching calculus to a cockroach. You just don't do it. "Something like that, a moment like that, is meant to be shared."

"I didn't share enough of myself with you last night?"

"Lily, that's not what I meant. I would have done things differently. I would have handled the situation differently."

She put her arms around my neck and pulled my head down until our foreheads were touching. "Julian, I didn't want to scare you. I'm sorry about that. I should have told you. But I want you to know something. Look at me. I want you to know that last night was my choice. I wanted to make love with my boyfriend for the first time last night. That was my birthday wish. I wanted to make love with you last night. Nothing else matters."

"You still should have told me."

"Yes, and it means a lot to me that you're upset about that. Not many guys would be." She kissed me. "Now, are we good?"

"We're good."

She smiled and released my neck but took hold of my hand and pulled. "I want my breakfast now."

"Okay. What sounds good?"

She turned and her mouth was on mine in an instant.

Clara sat at the dining room table with a glass of orange juice and a lit cigarette. When we finally emerged from our breakfast, she took one look at us, took a long drag, exhaled, and nodded as if in approval. Lily smiled sheepishly and looked down. I cleared my throat and mentioned the broken coffeemaker. Clara frowned.

I walked Lily to the door and kissed her goodbye.

Clara took a sip of juice when I reentered. "So how was your night?" she asked.

I took a seat and stole a sip. "Interesting."

"She actually a he?"

"No. A virgin."

Clara raised an eyebrow. "Interesting. How'd that go?"

I shrugged. "I don't know anything about women."

"An artful dodge."

An artful dodge? What had I dodged?

Like most any other couple, we were enraptured by each other's bodies. Every night, we explored, ferreting out the hidden patches of bare skin that responded with such exquisite pleasure to the lightest touch, the barest stroke. I discovered that a certain rub of her navel induced orgasm and that an upward lick along the ridge of her ear moistened her cleft like nothing else. She discovered that nails drawn sparingly across my back rendered me unable to speak and that bites along my shoulders caused my penis to spasm. Nighttime became a game of teasing denials, of erotic antagonisms every bit as stimulating as penetration. I introduced her to the many delights of covered genitals and bound hands, of ice cubes and champagne and candle wax. She was an eager pupil, aggressive and hungry for knowledge. I taught and demonstrated and she experienced and expanded upon. One night, as I brought an ice cube down between her breasts, she seized my hand and guided it between her thighs and pushed the ice cube inside her. Her head flew back and her body arched and her moan was something primal, but still she managed to me guide me into her and she came around both me and the melting ice cube as if evacuating her soul. I in turn came all the harder.

The quiet, simple moments between our delirious ecstasies belonged to Lily. I listened for hours to her thoughts and dreams and gossip and jokes and observations and lies and questions, and I sucked at this honey like a greedy fly. She could talk about reality television or politics or genetic engineering and I would lay there in a stupor, drunk off knowing she was speaking these things to me, that she wanted to be speaking these things to me. My eyes would go glassy with tears and Lily would pause and look at me and giggle and kiss me and the quiet would be broken.

During one such quiet, Lily asked if I was going to Ashley Park's funeral.

"I don't go to funerals anymore," I said, hoping rather foolishly she wouldn't pursue the matter.

"Why not?" she asked.

"There's nothing left to do at funerals after you've buried your own parents."

"What about showing sympathy for other people?"

"I buried my sympathy with my parents. They deserved it. I'm not sure why anyone else deserves it."

"Not even your students?"

"Ashley was a good kid. I really liked him. But I don't know his parents. I never met either of them, and what would I say? Gee, sorry about your son, that's some shit?"

"You know his friends. They'll be there. It would mean a lot to them to see you."

"What do I care about them? Ashley had some issues and clearly they didn't help…" I stopped.

Are you going to be here later?

"Julian?"

"Oh god."

"Julian, what's wrong?"

Can I talk to you afterwards?

"He wanted to talk to me after graduation. He was shaken up and I told him we'd talk after the ceremony. I forgot all about it. I just wanted to get out of there."

Lily lifted her head, started to say something, then lowered her head, and we lay in silence.

In the end, I went to the wake, not the funeral. Lily agreed to come with me. She hadn't known Ashley very well, but she was close to many of his friends. She said it was the least she could do for them and that she didn't want me going alone, though I suspect she worried I wouldn't go at all without someone to prod me along.

Ashley's family held the wake at the Dalton Brother's Funeral Parlor, a whitewashed building in the middle of one of Vesper's upper-class neighborhoods. The crowd was typical: boys in black suits that didn't quite fit correctly, girls in black dresses with skirts that were a tad too short and stilettos that were a tad too high, men who stood around chatting about the economy, women who stood around offering one another tissues. The casket was relatively simple, with a textured, rose-colored metal finish. The family opted to keep it closed, for obvious reasons, but standing in front of it while muttering a few words to a deity I didn't believe in, I wondered if there was any piece of Ashley inside. After the car accident, the mortician suggested we cremate the bodies and hold a fake funeral with two empty caskets. She said it would be easier on us financially and emotionally. She said it wasn't crass. She said all this in the tone of an infinitely patient Labrador retriever. What did the mortician say to Ashley's parents? What were they shown when they arrived at the morgue? Did they recognize the corpse as their son?

Ashley's mother clasped my hands in hers and wailed about how much he enjoyed having me as his teacher, and what could I say in response to that? She shook my hands and behind her mourning veil waited for me to share in her grief. I could only shake my head and mouth, "I'm sorry." She hugged me and wailed in my ear and her husband placed a hand on her back and took her from me with a nod and a quiet "Thank you." Lily placed a hand on my back and led me away.

I waited in the coatroom for fifteen minutes while Lily said her goodbyes. Outside, she held my hand and said, "I'm glad you came. I know that was hard for you." When I didn't respond, she said, "I'm sorry. I didn't mean to upset you." Silence. "I've never asked. How did your parents die?"

I could have told her, but I didn't.

The next morning, Principal Hunter woke me by pounding on the front door. I answered in my robe.

"Morning, Maddy," I said. "Kinda early, isn't it?"

132

"Julian, we need to talk."

"About?"

"Can I come in?"

"No. What do we need to talk about?"

"You and Miss Carter."

"I haven't had my coffee yet. What do you mean?"

"I mean, are you sleeping with Lily Carter?"

"That's really none of your business."

"It's all over town and the Internet that you are, so yes, it is actually my business. Now, are you sleeping with her or not?"

"Maddy, I am not going to answer that."

"Because the answer's yes or because the answer's no? Julian, are you having sex with her?"

"Perhaps you didn't understand me. Would you like me to repeat myself in Latin?"

"Answer the damn question!"

"Go to hell!"

"Julian, are you fucking Lily Carter or not?"

"Yes! Yes, I'm fucking her all the time! I fuck her every chance I get! I fuck her everywhere we go, up to and including on the desk in my classroom! When you leave, I'm going to fuck her brains out because I haven't fucked her yet this morning! Would you like to come in and say hi before I do?!"

Principal Hunter stuck a finger in my face. "Julian, if the board gets wind of this, there's…" She dropped her finger and shook her head. "You need to end this right now. I don't know how you could be so goddamn stupid, but it needs to end immediately."

"Get the fuck off my property. Right now. My personal life does not belong to you or the board or the district. I have done nothing wrong."

"Do you really think that's going to matter to anyone?"

I slammed the door.

"That was really fucking stupid of you," Clara said from behind me.

"Clara, don't start with me."

"Julian, in four years, has that woman been anything but supportive

133

of you? Do you really think it's a good idea to alienate someone who has always had your back?"

I turned. "Jesus Christ, Clara! I…"

Lily stood in the bedroom doorway, white as the sheet wrapped around her body.

"Julian?"

Clara looked at Lily, then at me, and sighed. "Come on, sweetie. Let me make you some eggs."

Clara took Lily by the shoulders and walked into the dining room. Lily went with her but not before turning to give me a look of desperation.

I shrugged and opened my mouth to reassure her, but there was nothing.

Chapter 11
New Year's Prayer

We had been unbelievably stupid, going to the wake together and never considering that someone might ask why and jump to the right conclusion. Lily ate and then spent the rest of the morning in my bed, crying then sleeping then waking to cry some more. I spent the morning scouring the Internet for every mention of Lily and me. It took all of fifteen seconds before the search engine filled my browser with Vespers' latest obsession.

Rendezvous had been created by people who didn't know either of us. Sexual acts had been imagined and detailed for the world to read. Suddenly, it seemed we really had been fucking everywhere, and someone had always been there to bear witness to our depravity. Surprisingly, only a fraction of the commentary was directed at me. I was a perverse old man but few seemed to care. Lily, on the other hand, had become the whore of Vespers.

OMG MR SANE IS SCREWING LILY CARTER!!!!!
#PERVYTEACHER
Julian Sane pays his students to fuck him.
I GOT THERE FIRST SANE! #SLOPPYSECONDS
LilyCarter is a ugly slut he can have her

Lily likes to suck diseased cock

I saw them fingerbanging in the park!

I hope they filmed it sometime

Thousands more followed. We had become the sport of the season, and there was nothing we could do about it. When had this all happened? I tried to imagine Stephanie Shoulders whipping out her iPhone and mass texting her contact list, but I couldn't get from that moment to the endless commentary scrolling through my browser. If she informed every last student in the high school, that only amounted to 400 people. Who was left for those 400 to tell? Who else cared about a sex scandal involving the dirty English teacher? But even if each of those 400 only told two other people, the exponential growth would have overtaken the town within days. Judging from the sheer volume of comments, that was exactly what had happened.

But who were these people? The students I could understand. The chance to talk smack about one of their teachers was not something even the best behaved would pass up. The bulk of the commentary, however, did not come from students. The overwhelming majority came from people who had never met me, people who most likely had never even heard of me except maybe in some vague connection to the school.

I tried to reason through the chain of events. Stephanie told her friends. Who did they tell? They told each other, so the gossip bounced around the same group for a day or two and then disappeared once they lost interest. Clearly, someone else had to have entered the network. A parent, perhaps? Teenagers don't talk to their parents for the most part, not about anything of substance, but it was conceivable a parent could have overheard part of a phone conversation. Would the parent then have repeated what he overheard? The right parent, yes, one who did not like me—there were plenty of those—and one who knew enough people to start a fire. This could have tripled the number of people talking, which would have substantially increased the odds of someone in no way connected with the school hearing about the matter.

I sighed. Confectioners discussing Lily and me while baking. Old women discussing us at the hair salon. Whole congregations discussing us before mass. Was it really so absurd a notion? Wherever two or more people gathered, was it merely a spin of the wheel whether they were talking about us?

Apparently so. But what was their interest? What exactly had we done? We were two adults engaged in a consensual relationship. We weren't fucking each other. We were dating. We enjoyed each other's company. We talked and laughed and shared and, yes, we were having sex on a regular basis, just like any other couple. Was it the age difference, the eleven years between us? Was it how we had first met each other? Was it because the moon was waning or because the tide was high or because MCA had died? No one gave any real indication what the issue was, but they all took their turns flogging us for it. Even if there was something to apologize for, no one would let up long enough for either of us to do so. The great, unforgiving mob. All we could do was bury our heads in the sand and hope for a reprieve.

When Lily finally came out of the bedroom, she was fully clothed and she headed straight for the front door. I caught her and held her and said I was sorry, but she kept pushing away and wiping at her eyes. Was it my fault? Clara had tried to warn me, but I wouldn't listen. She said it would end in tears. Maybe I thought we'd have a longer grace period. Maybe I thought I'd be the only one punished. What did that matter to the woman in my arms struggling to get away from me?

She fought me off and ran out the door, only to collapse in tears against the side of her car. I asked Clara to drive Lily home, and she did so without a word of response.

I didn't see Lily or speak with her for the next three days.

If she needed space, I understood. If she needed time to decide what our newfound notoriety meant, I understood. If she needed escape from the confines of reality, I understood. What I couldn't understand was her retreat from me, as if I had somehow caused this. I would drive past her house and see her through the windows, but then she would see me and pull the drapes and I would remember exactly what it was like to be eighteen. Drama, drama, so much drama. It didn't help that this was actual drama cooked up by malcontent redneck assholes to amuse themselves in between benders. How did we not see this coming? What did we think was going to happen?

We had been living in a delirium, ignorant of everything except each other. What else could love be but a haze dropped upon everything and everyone save for thee and thine? Where was the crunch of gravel beneath my feet, the pink glow along the ridges of clouds in the first minutes of sunrise, the warm, sugary scent of the chocolate factory? What happened to the dry sound of wind blowing through the wheat fields? Did the world stop for us or did we stop the world? Ridiculous. Nothing disappears just because two people forget to notice it. A tree falls in the forest and it generates sound waves, even in the absence of any creature able to experience said waves. I can turn my back upon a whole city, but that city remains. It endures. It flourishes. Whether I'm aware of it or not, life goes on.

Clara offered little in the way of consolation beyond keeping the liquor cabinet well stocked. Whenever I tried talking to her, she would make an excuse to lock herself in her bedroom with a case of Schlitz and a stereo at full volume. What was she hiding from? The fact that her baby brother had done a bad, bad thing? The knowledge that she had been right and yet had done nothing to prevent the situation? I didn't blame my sister any more than I blamed Lily.

Principal Hunter leaned back in her chair, folded her hands together, and gazed out the window, the slightest smile on her lips.

"Well?" I asked.

Her eyelids fluttered, but she said nothing. I reached forward and tapped a finger on her desk. The sound was flat in the office and disappeared almost immediately. I sat back and ran a hand through my hair. Principal Hunter continued to gaze out the window as if the passing cars were the most delightful thing she had ever known.

When she finally spoke, her voice was lower than usual, with a ringing like funeral bells. "I could tell you to get the fuck out of my office."

"You could."

She swiveled in her chair to face me, then leaned her elbows on the desk. "Dr. Mengoweitz is gathering the board members to him."

Try not to sound so excited. "And?"

She smiled. "He wants you gone."

"And what does the rest of the board want?"

"They want to keep their seats."

Typical bureaucrats. "And my personal life is going to be their campaign platform. Is that it?"

"Mr. Sane, your dick just got you in a whole lot of trouble. I'm not sure you have the proper appreciation for just how much trouble you're about to experience."

"Madeline, my girlfriend is totally ignoring me and my sister is trying to drink herself into a coma. Believe me when I say that I can appreciate the trouble in which I currently find myself."

She leaned back. "That is not going to help you. That smug indignation, like you did nothing wrong. You're having a sexual relationship with one of your students."

"Former, and she was never actually a student of mine."

"You're being intentionally naïve. You and I both know it's the perception that people care about."

"I'm not breaking up with her."

"You do not have a choice."

"Oh, yes, I do. I will not have my life dictated to me by a bunch of suits who think they own me simply because they gave me a job."

"Those suits are going to fire you for this. Whether they want to or not, they will fire you to save face."

"Then let them fire me."

"Is that what you really want? Because the board is going to claim moral turpitude and sexual misconduct, and let me tell you something about what happens to teachers who are fired for that: they never work in education again. No school anywhere is going to hire a teacher who may or may not have violated the teacher-student relationship. No school. Anywhere. You will be finished in education, to say nothing of, I have no idea how you'd get a job doing anything since you'd have to explain your dismissal to potential employers. Who's going to hire you if you can't keep your dick in your pants and can't be discreet about it? You will be done, Julian. You will be done."

"Do you think I should be fired for this?"

"Julian, what I think is irrelevant."

"I'm not asking employee to employer. I'm asking as one person to another: do you believe I should be fired for this?"

She was silent. Then she turned to the window and said, "I don't think it's fair to tell a person who he can or cannot care about. But this is a business, and fairness does not enter into it."

I stood. "You're a real fucking cunt, you know that?"

And I walked out of her office, not even bothering to slam the door.

Friday night. 10:00 PM. 6925 kHz USB. Three pounds of a gavel, followed by "The Star-Spangled Banner" played on a toy piano, followed by the opening of Depeche Mode's "Never Let Me Down Again," ending immediately following the first drum hit.

Then the baritone voice: "Good evening, friends and lovers. This is Midnight coming to you live for the next several hours on *Pomegranate Radio*: pirate radio for the masses. I'd like to dedicate our first song tonight to a very special couple. It seems one of our local teachers has been tupping a pretty white student. Hell, this is the land of the free, so I say tup away without shame. Mr. Sane, this one's for you and that delicate flower you've deflowered. Ladies and gentlemen, teachers and students: 'New Year's Prayer.'"

Rumors could be ignored, comments on Facebook or Twitter dismissed, but *Pomegranate Radio* spoke the truth. Never mind that it was a half-baked version of the truth or that it ignored any sense of context. Midnight had spoken and his judgment stood. Let spectators greet me on this, my day of execution, with cries of hate.

Clara scrambled a few eggs and fried potatoes and we ate in silence and dark. Afterward, we sat on the living room floor and went over the final draft of Clara's play. I suggested a bit of polish for the occasional phrase, but nothing absolutely necessary. Clara's months of drafting had yielded a minor dramatic masterpiece that identified its strengths early on and played to them without shame.

The play unfolds as a series of alternating confessions told by a college freshman and a middle-aged lawyer to an elderly priest. In the first confession, the freshman details how she met the lawyer after a speaking engagement at the college. After a long evening of drinks and conversation, the two parted, but the lawyer followed the freshman back to her dormitory and assaulted her in the basement laundry room. His attempted rape was interrupted by a janitor and he fled from the building after a brief struggle in which he received a black eye. The priest urges the freshman to report the attack, but she refuses, saying nothing happened to warrant putting herself through what would come of her report. The next confession details the lawyer's point of view. He confesses to following the freshman back to her dormitory, but claims she taunted him in the laundry room repeatedly after insinuating her desire for him. In his anger, he slapped her, at which point she began hitting him and he struggled to fend off her blows. The lawyer admits the janitor acted in perfect fairness to the situation he saw. The priest urges the lawyer to make amends to the freshman, and the lawyer agrees.

The next two confessions occur two weeks later. In the freshman's, we learn how the lawyer caught up to her several days after their first incident in a park and succeeded in raping her. The priest urges the freshman to report the rape, but she refuses, saying she does not know whether she was horrified or enjoyed the experience and therefore cannot be certain she holds the lawyer at fault. The priest does not understand this and again presses her to report the lawyer, at which point the freshman leaves in silence. The lawyer, speaking a day later, explains how he went to apologize for his actions during the first incident only to have the freshman tease him

141

with suggestions of a sexual rendezvous in the park. The lawyer rebuffed her advances and she became irate, threatening to report him for sexual assault. The lawyer says he left shortly thereafter.

The following confession takes place three days later. The freshman details breaking into the lawyer's home and torturing him in order to extract a taped confession. The lawyer repeatedly refused, and her methods grew more and more sadistic, from beating him with a metal dildo to breaking his fingers one by one with a small hammer. When the lawyer finally admitted to raping her, she ordered him to call his mother and confess to her. He refused and she beat him into unconsciousness with a cane. The priest is shocked and demands she turn herself over to the police. She refuses, saying she finally understands why a rapist rapes.

In the final confession, the elderly priest admits to a much younger priest that he broke the confessional seal by going to the police. The young priest denies him absolution and chastises the elderly priest for violating his sacred duty. The elderly priest begins to cry and asks, "Does God forgive beasts their actions, or does He forgive men alone?" Then the curtain falls.

Clara's working title was *The Ecstasy of St. Francis.* I suggested *The Book of Hours*, which she ultimately settled on, though whether she did so because the title was inherently superior or because she pitied my situation, I still do not know.

When we finished, Clara poured me a Scotch and made her one concession to my plight. "You need to get yourself a lawyer," she said.

A woman appeared at my door the next morning and handed me a white business card: Jamie Brays, *The Daily Freedom.* I dropped the card and waited.

"Do you have any comment on the school board's recent decision to terminate your employment?" she asked.

I reached into my pocket, removed my cell phone, and dialed Principal Hunter. She answered on the second ring.

"Maddy, I have a reporter at my door asking me to comment on the school board's decision to terminate my employment. Is there something you need to tell me?"

Principal Hunter sighed. "A special meeting has been called for next week to discuss the matter."

"Discuss the matter or publically humiliate me before firing me?"

The reporter raised a tape recorder and pressed the red button. I slammed the door in her face.

"Does it really matter at this point, Julian? You've already made your choice."

"And they've made their decision. The meeting is a formality."

"They cannot officially make their decision before the meeting."

"Officially."

"Julian."

"Madeline, is there any way to get out of this with my balls intact?"

"No."

Chapter 12
Raise Your Weapon

There was a solution to our problem. It was a victory for the puritans who deemed us sinners, but it was also an escape from those assholes. All I had to do was break up with Lily, tell her we were never going to work and that the pain our relationship had brought us was not worth a fleeting bit of pleasure. All I had to say was that I didn't love her, that I had never loved her, that I never could love her. Why not? The community outrage would settle down and I might be able to keep my job. At the very least, I would be permitted to exit with my dignity intact and never have to answer embarrassing questions about my wandering penis. But what of Lily? Could I say those things to her and watch the confusion turn to anger and misery? How would I stand up against her eyes pleading with me to reconsider, to hold her, to love her? What man is a man when his lover touches him in sorrow and agony? What man would not burn cities into ash to spare someone he loves even a moment of unpleasantness?

I couldn't hurt her. Damn the masses! Let them come to my door with pitchforks and tar! I would not yield to a madding crowd of savages who denied anything could exist outside of their experience. Let them judge me a sinner! Let them hate me and strip me and crucify me! Let them take my job and my career! I would not bow to base animals who preached love for all but decried the Muslim as a threat to the kingdom of Heaven and the homosexual as an abomination in the eyes of God. Let them pile tinder at my feet and set me to burn! I would not deny her.

What nobility there would be in that! Yet, what man could throw himself so willingly upon the sword? What man would not wish to spare himself the agony of so great a fall? What is the value of man's honor in modern currency? Shame be damned! I was a coward. I was a fool standing before a tidal wave, believing my righteous indignation would hold the waters at bay. What is a man against the faceless chaos of a mob? To live is to suffer in the hope that one does not suffer in vain. What reasonable hope could be held?

My hands, my clean, pink hands, lined but untouched by scars or callouses, hands that held Lily to me, hands that explored the recesses of her body and extracted from them all manner of ecstasy. Had these hands violated? Had they preyed upon and vitiated my sometime ward? With these hands, I loved her. With these hands, I would hold her and protect her and wipe away the tears of judgment. If these hands could be forgiven, what they would do for her!

I was to blame. A schoolgirl crush ignored is soon forgotten and replaced by some other trivial fancy. I had cultivated hers, nurtured it until we had no choice but to entwine ourselves in love's duet. She was intoxicating, her beauty, her youth, her innocence. But beauty fades, youth comes to an end, and all innocence is corrupted. How could she forgive me that?

She came well after dark, sneaking in as Clara left for a late-night drink on the square and standing in perfect quiet in the living room. Then came a hastened breathing, a staccato intake of breath, and a soft sobbing. She stood with outstretched arms and I ran to her and held her tight against the gathering night. "Make love to me," she pleaded, and in her plea, all was forgiven because nothing mattered anymore. Our bodies ached for closure like they ached for sunlight, and we coiled around each other until we were satiated by sweat and tears.

Later, after exhaustion won out over Lily's desire for a few moments more, I confessed myself to her slumbering form, and in her repose, she smiled.

"I love you, Lily."

I snuck a pinch of Clara's weed from the bandage tin beneath the sink, rolled a joint, and sat down at my computer.

My Dearest Lily,

Nothing in the world has given me greater joy than being able to know you as I have. I can never give back all you've given to me, nor can I offer anything in return to equal it. But know that I love you very much, more so than I'm capable of saying. I locked myself away so I would never have to know what comes after falling in love. It's a fear all children harbor, that those they love will not love them, and if you do requite my love, I count myself all the more blessed.

But there is no place for us. I can't stand to see your unhappiness and know I'm the cause of it. I can't ask you to build something with me if everyone who sees it will want to destroy it. You should be above such sacrifice. You should be with a man who would raze the people for you. I so wish I were that man, but I know I'm not now and never will be. I'm a coward and a fool, all the more for ever believing I could love you the way you deserve to be loved.

I'm sorry, Lily. I am so very sorry.

Love,

J

I printed a copy, checked it over for phraseology, then folded it into an envelope. I scrawled her name across the front in large letters, then set it aside while I finished smoking the joint. It wasn't a noble thing, the letter. It wasn't dignified and it wasn't worthy of a man, but it was the best I could offer her. The path of least pain. I would set it on my pillow and be gone before morning. I'd drive into the country and waste the day kicking patches of dirt in open fields with my phone off. In the darkness,

I'd come back to find an empty bed still possessed by the lingering scent of her skin. There would be phone calls for awhile, voice messages begging for a response, but each one would be easier to ignore than the last. In a few weeks' time, Lily would be nothing but a fond memory, and after a few weeks more, she wouldn't even be that.

I had a plan, and it was a solid plan right up to the moment I placed the envelope on the pillow. Lily rolled over in her sleep and reached out an arm that met mine, startling her awake.

She blinked, and even her narcotic stupor couldn't hide her suspicion that something was amiss. "Julian?" she asked.

I pulled back and stood against the wall with my hands in the pockets of my robe. "Hello" was all I could manage.

"What's wrong?" She looked at the envelope lying beside her. "You're breaking up with me." It wasn't a question.

"Yes," I said with no small amount of shame and embarrassment.

A kind of calm descended upon her features. She sat up, tucking the sheets beneath her arms. "Why?"

"You know why."

"Say it."

"Lily—"

"Say it!"

"Because it was a mistake."

"Because they're going to label you the teacher who fucks his students."

"Don't talk like that, Lily. It was never about the sex."

She sniffled. "Just like you cared about my virginity. What was that, Julian? Did it sound just dramatic enough to earn you points? Or did you just think it was what needed to be said at that moment? That meant so much to me, for the first man I ever slept with to get so worked up over the fact that he was my first. Was that all a lie?"

No. "Yes. When I realized you were a virgin, I figured you would need comforting or some shit like that."

Her eyes welled up. "How can you say that? All this time... did you ever care about me?"

Yes. "I enjoyed fucking you. But come on, Lily. You knew this wouldn't

147

last."

The tears were rolling down her cheeks. "No. No, I didn't know that. If you knew, you could have told me. But you didn't."

I said nothing.

She gave a desperate chuckle. "Why did you do this?"

Because I love you. "Because I was bored and needed some kind of amusement to pass the summer months. Thank you for that, by the way."

"You're unbelievable."

"I get that a lot."

"Do you care at all that you were the first man I ever slept with?"

Yes. "You weren't my first. Hell sweetheart, you weren't even in the first twenty. It's not that big of a deal."

She froze. Her eyes locked on mine and then looked down and darted about the bed. Her breathing sped up and trembled. She began to turn from side to side as if searching for something. "Okay," she said. She began running her hands across the sheets, lifting here and there. "Okay. I need to find…" She continued searching, her breathing growing more labored and her mouth twisting into a rictus of agony.

"Lily—"

"*GET OUT!*" she howled with all the fury of hell. One was all she had in her, but one was all she needed. Her face turned pale scarlet and purple. Her eyes collapsed into heaps of flesh. Tears flowed freely. Her mouth was a wide O from which came sporadic, cough-like sounds. She clutched her abdomen and rocked forward as if punched repeatedly.

I walked out of the bedroom and shut the door behind me. The thing in my bed was my creation, and there I was fleeing from it like Viktor Frankenstein. I no longer wanted her forgiveness. I wanted her hatred, her absolute, unconditional hatred, for that was the only thing I deserved.

By the time she left, I was slumped in the corner of the dining room dead drunk.

Chapter 13
Cars Go By

Clara slapped me until the slaps stopped stinging. I raised the envelope between the two of us and wobbled unsteadily. She snatched it from my hand, shook it, then threw it in my face. All the while she screamed, "You son of a bitch! You fucker! Why did you do that?"

"I needed to get rid of her. I did what was best for her."

"What was best for her? You really are an asshole! That wasn't a breakup! It was sadism! You don't gut a woman to keep her away from you! You don't skewer her simply because it's effective!"

I put up no defense. What defense could I give? I had been cruel, perhaps needlessly so, to a woman whose only crime had been collusion with a man who should have known better. I deserved wrath. I deserved pain. I deserved humiliation.

How quickly these things happen! A man wakes to find a beautiful woman watching him sleep, he falls for her and she for him, and then the real world intervenes with a swift and terrible justice. Balance is restored. We are so small, an atom in a grain of sand on a beach at the end of the world, and we are so easily dismissed. A single kick can send us screaming into the oblivion of an ocean, where we drown without the water ever taking notice of us. Or we suffer. We justify our existence by saying the world is a different place for our having been in it, but what do we do? What do we leave that is not washed away? What trace remains of the billions who have lived and died upon this rock? Our lives are the sum total of our existence, and what do they matter? Our stupid, little lives. We know we live because we affect others, yet there has been more suffering imposed than love shared throughout history, and because it ever has been thus, ever shall it be thus.

Could I excuse my failings as a man? What is the measure of a man? Is it the fill of his trousers and the spread of his seed? Or is it his capacity to stand against armies and to love those who stab him? I had attacked one I loved merely to spare myself ridicule. I was a beast, a beast of no breeding and no conviction, a beast of pure self-preservation, and a beast is a beast, not a man. Never a man.

Clara refused to stand by me. She said what I had done to Lily was unforgivable. She said she was returning to Chicago as soon as possible. "I'm ashamed of you," she said, "and you should be ashamed of yourself. I know mom and dad would be."

I agreed with everything she said.

The days melted together.

The snickers could be heard while at the grocery store or the post office. Whispers behind indiscreet hands at restaurants. Sudden hushes wherever my presence added to the two or more people gathered. The brief nod of heads in my direction: there he is. And worst of all, the stares, the brazen, shameless stares between gas pumps, across streets, through windows. How the people do love a scandal!

As soon as word of the board meeting got around, the newspaper ran an editorial calling for my immediate dismissal. I was dangerous, it said. It called me "a vicious reminder of the power we as parents surrender when dropping our children off at school" and went on to blame me "for the drop in our high school's academic performance. With teachers like Mr. Sane on staff—and he cannot possibly be the only one of his kind on staff—it is a miracle our children are doing as well as they are. What we need is a sweep of the high school, a public, top-to-bottom analysis of everything going on in every classroom so that parents are aware of the risks they make in sending their children to Vespers Community High School."

Responses ran every day and labeled me a pedophile, a child molester, a monster. "Mr. Sane has blatantly abused his position as a teacher for prurient ends and must be punished accordingly," one letter read. "If it was up to me, I'd strip him of his job and his degrees. There is no place in decent society for men like him." The worst were the letters that made up stories about my inequities: "My daughter told me that every time she had Mr. Sane, he had this look in his eye. Now I wonder if he wasn't planning to seduce my little girl." Or: "I went in for a conference with Mr. Sane to discuss my daughter's grade. When he shook my hand, he just kept holding on and rubbing me and I swear he looked like he was getting off on it." My personal favorite was from my neighbor: "I've caught Sane peeping through my window at my wife five or six times. He denies it every time I confront him about it, but my wife says she's afraid to be alone in the house now that she knows how sick he is."

Only one letter defending me was run. James Pfister, a student of mine who had graduated in May, wrote it. "Mr. Sane was not only the best teacher I ever had at VCHS but also the most dedicated. He pushed his students, all of us, to go beyond our own thoughts and see issues from different angles. I didn't agree with everything he made us consider, but that wasn't the point. He wanted his students to understand different views so we could better understand why we believe what we believe. Some of his methods were unconventional, and he tried a lot of different teaching methods, but he always had a reason for what he did. He always explained why we were studying something, which not one of my other teachers ever did. All of this is to say, I can't see any grounds for his being dismissed as far as his job is concerned. As for his personal life, it's just that: his personal life. No one has any right to tell him how to live his life, so leave him alone."

I cut out James' letter and pinned it to the wall above my computer.

James hated my class because I kept telling him his Works Cited entries were incorrect. He would try to correct them but instead make them worse, and I would throw up my hands and begin ranting about using his MLA guide. He got it right eventually, though, and on graduation night, he shook my hand and told me he really did enjoy my class even if I was mean sometimes. Now he was coming to my defense. Maybe I wasn't such a shitty teacher after all.

I tried to focus on the positive, on my one letter of defense, but I kept coming back to the number: one. One letter of defense. Maybe it was simply easier for everyone to vilify me.

I went to The Disintegration Room alone for the first time in months. Garbo poured a gin and tonic as soon as he saw me and set it on the bar. "On the house, man," he said with the kind of sincerity only bartenders possess. Then he poured himself one and waited for me to sit.

I drank it down in one long gulp.

Garbo raised a brow. "The first one's free, man. The rest ya gotta pay for."

"My money's still good. They haven't fired me yet."

He chuckled. "Shouldn't ya be saving yer nickels and dimes fer lean times?"

"Fuck lean times. Fuck the board. Fuck the district. Fuck America!" I pounded my fist on the bar. Several patrons looked my way. I grinned and waved. "Just kidding." I raised my tumbler. "Fuck the Muslims!" That got a round of cheers and raised glasses. I turned back to Garbo. "Think they know any Muslims?"

Garbo took a drink. "Yer in deep shit, kid. Seriously deep shit. Ya might wanna start rethinking yer approach."

I tapped the tumbler and he poured another.

"Okay, Garbo. What would you do? If you were me, what would you do?"

He scratched at his nose. "I'd suck off ev'ry swinging dick on that board."

152

"Garbo, that's because you're both a fag and a slut."

"Julie, my boy, ya really gonna call me a slut? How many women I seen ya leave with since ya started coming here?"

I raised my tumbler. "Cheers to that. And look what it's gotten me."

"It could be worse. Yer penis could be rotting off."

"There's always that." I took a sip. "Do you think I was wrong?"

He waved goodbye to a young couple as they left. "Who the fuck cares if ya were wrong? Ya did it. It's done. Most people are throwing a fit 'cause they wish they were the one fucking her. Including that supreme asshole trying to cut yer balls off."

"Mengoweitz?"

"That dude's a grade-A douche. Take a guess how many times I've had to boot his self-righteous ass outta here."

"He's Mormon. I didn't think they could drink."

"Never seems to stop him. And he's a mean-ass drunk. I told him last time he was in here, If ya touch my girls one more time, I'm gonna snap yer fingers off and store 'em with the dill pickles."

I grinned. "What did he say?"

"Fucker muttered something about Christ hating my faggot ass. Shit, I go to church ev'ry Sunday, too. I ain't goin' burn in hell."

"Well, if you do, you'll be in good company. That's where all the interesting people are." I raised my tumbler. "To burning in hell!"

Despite his admonishing me to pay for my own drinks, Garbo kept pouring, so I kept drinking. After awhile, it no longer mattered that the board wanted me dead or that I had broken up with my girlfriend because other people didn't like our dating each other. I forgot the profit and the loss, and I was happy.

At some point, Sammy the tattoo artist made his nightly call to ply his trade on unsuspecting drunks for the amusement of the slightly less intoxicated drunks. Because Clara wasn't there to temper the impulse, I raised my arm in a heuristic gesture and asked if he could ink me with a sewer rat raising its rat fist in unadulterated rage from behind the bars of a cage. He said he could.

That night, I kept reaching in my sleep for Lily. When my arm fell upon nothing but air where I expected her body to be, I snapped awake and looked around in confusion. Then I'd close my eyes and try to sleep.

When I did manage to sleep, I dreamt of Lily standing in my living room in a white, floor-length nightgown. She reached out to me, but no matter how hard I ran, I couldn't reach her. A crimson stained appeared in the center of her nightgown and slowly spread outwards.

I started early Saturday morning.

Shirley Betts, social worker for the Department of Child and Family Services. Married. Two children. One Rottweiler. I thought the dog was going to tear through the door until Betts shooed it away.

As soon as I introduced myself, her smile faded and she demanded to know what I wanted. I explained that with the topic of the upcoming board meeting, I wanted a chance to discuss the situation with her so she could make an informed decision. She threatened to call the police if I ever knocked on her door again.

After she slammed the door in my face, I knocked again and ran.

Payton Harold Cather-Pittnum III, lawyer. With a name like his, what else could he have been? Divorced. No children. Southern accent. He shook my hand with both of his before ushering me into his home. We sat in plush chairs and ate scones and drank sweet tea in what he called the drawing room but was really just an oversized spare bedroom.

"Sir, the reason I'm here is because the board has been given an impression of my situation and I wanted to give you my side of the story so you can make the most informed decision possible."

He raised a hand. "Mr. Sane, I'm going to stop you right there. I have no intention of going along with Dr. Mengoweitz' preposterous witch-hunt. If someone were to demonstrate mental incompetence or bring charges of impropriety within your classroom, that would be one thing. This nonsense of accusing you of sexual misconduct is obscene. You have the right in this great country to bed whomever you so choose. Your girlfriend is not a minor, nor is she currently your student or a student of VCHS. It may be unseemly for you to be dating her, but something being unseemly is not and never has been grounds for dismissal."

When he finished, I almost stood up and applauded. "Thank you. I'm very glad to hear you say all that. I just hope other board members feel the same way."

He shook his head. "Betts won't. She's a bitch. O'Neill might, but he's afraid of Mengoweitz, so probably not. Ditto for Morris and Slaren. Stephens' daughter was raped by a black man, so she sees sexual deviancy in everything. She's out. That just leaves me and Mengoweitz, and Alastair wants you dead."

"So if I get him, I'll be able to keep my job?" I asked.

"Mr. Sane, you won't get him. He doesn't like you."

"Why not? That's what I don't understand. Why is this such a big deal?"

"Because he's up for reelection next year. You're going to be his campaign."

"So I'm fucked. Sorry. So I'm screwed."

"Pretty much. My guess is, if you show some contrition, apologize and whatnot, tell the board you made a mistake and deeply regret it, blah blah blah, Alastair'll give you the chance to resign your position. At least then you won't be fired."

"I'll still have a career."

"You'll still have a career. I'm sorry, Mr. Sane. I surely am. Prior to this, I'd never heard anything but positive things about you."

"I don't suppose you want to be my lawyer."

"Conflict of interest, my boy. Conflict of interest."

I stood, shook his hand, and turned to leave, but he caught my arm.

"Can I ask you one thing before you go?" he asked.

I nodded.

"What made you do it? Date her, I mean. Why bother? You had to know it would end badly. For both of you."

155

I thought about it. "I was shitfaced and she found me and took me home because she was worried about what would happen to me. And she didn't care that I was shitfaced. She was just worried about my safety. And she never threw it back at me."

He nodded. "Love makes sinners of us all."

I smiled and thanked him for the tea and scones. He invited me to come back and visit him any time. He promised he would do what he could on his end but admitted it wouldn't be much. At least he was willing to try.

And he did serve excellent scones.

I knew what I had to do. Speaking with the individual board members was only going to lead to more doors being slammed in my face. Most of them were puppets, so I had to speak with the puppet master. I had to see Dr. Alastair Mengoweitz. If he wanted me gone, I was gone, but if I could convince him I wasn't any kind of threat to the safety and sanctity of the community, I might survive.

Mengoweitz lived in a subdivision just north of the town limits, one of those gated communities where every home costs well over $500,000. Christ! In a town the size of Vespers, who builds a house that costs half a million dollars? I had to be registered as a guest by a security guard who wasn't wearing a gun or a nightstick but nevertheless managed to sound intimidating. He gave me a badge to wear and a placard for my windshield. Maybe the Occupy Wall Street assholes had a point after all. He directed me to a specific visitor parking zone and gave me directions from there to Mengoweitz' home, a garish monstrosity with Roman columns flanking the pink stone walkway leading from the sidewalk to the front porch.

His Aston Martin was parked in the driveway, a glittering reminder to everyone from his neighbors to his paperboy that he had made it in the world. The longer I looked at it, the more I wished someone would drive it into the Wabash River, and I wondered how much it would cost to hire someone to do that.

I rang the doorbell. No response. I rang again. I knocked. I knocked harder. I started to walk around to the back, but the door finally opened.

Paul Mengoweitz, the youngest son, stared at me.

"Hello," I said.

He kept staring. Apparently, money can't buy social grace.

"My name is Mr. Sane. Can I speak with your father?"

Mengoweitz came hurrying up behind Paul. "I'll deal with this, son. Go inside and help your mother with the dishes."

Paul kept staring at me and didn't leave until his father placed a hand on his shoulder and guided him back into the house.

Mengoweitz turned back to me and stuck his hands in his pockets. "Yes?"

I cleared my throat and chewed back my pride. "Dr. Mengoweitz, I wondered if we could talk for a few minutes about my situation."

"Mr. Sane, I don't see that we have anything to talk about."

I lowered my head and tried to look penitent. "I understand the position I've put the district in, and I'd like to apologize to you for that."

"Oh?"

"I realize how I've embarrassed the high school, the district, and the board, and I'd like to—"

"Mr. Sane, the embarrassment to our school district your actions have caused is the least of my concerns. You have grotesquely misused your position as an educator. You have preyed upon a child in our district. Mr. Sane, you are a troubled individual who has no right to be anywhere near our students."

"I understand where you are coming from, sir, but I do not agree with your characterization of my relationship with Miss Carter. It was a consensual relationship. Miss Carter and I each made a decision to engage in this relationship. It was a mistake, I admit. I displayed very poor judgment."

"Your poor judgment means nothing to me. You cavorted with a girl significantly younger than yourself. I am more concerned with the trauma such an experience put Miss Carter through."

"Sir, I may not be the noblest man in the world, but dating me is hardly traumatic."

"You are going to make a joke of this? Do you think this is funny? Mr.

Sane, your misconduct is appalling. Your actions have scarred that young lady for the rest of her life. Do you have any idea the psychic torment she will suffer when she tries to engage in a legitimate relationship later in life? Did you ever consider the consequences of your poor choices? Mr. Sane, your behavior is despicable, and I will not have you further sully the reputation of our district by allowing you to remain in our employ."

"Psychic torment?"

"In other words, the long-term consequences of having her trust in you so egregiously violated."

"So you've already made your decision. You're going to fire me."

"Mr. Sane, you made our decision for us when you decided to engage in an illicit relationship with a child under your care."

"And the truth doesn't matter to you. Be sure to include that in your campaign literature."

"Mr. Sane, you need to leave. Your presence here is inappropriate and unwanted."

I turned to go. "If you do this, I'll call every news outlet in the country and tell them my version of the truth. You'll have made me a motherfucking rock star and yourself a little asshole in a pissant redneck town."

He leaned closer to me. "Mr. Sane, I wish you had been fucking your mother. That way—"

He didn't finish. His nose shattered immediately upon contact with my fist. Two spurts of blood shot out of his nostrils and stained his light blue polo shirt. He collapsed with his hands to his nose and he squealed incoherently.

"My mother's dead, asshole."

Mengoweitz rocked back and forth. "So are you, Sane," he said through his hands. "Call whoever you want, but you'll never work in education again."

"Maybe not, but you'll always be the asshole whose nose I broke."

I left him there knowing I had just fucked myself over, but no one talks shit about my family.

* * * *

"So that's the score," I said to the headstones. "One board member basically told me to go fuck myself, another told me he was powerless to change anyone's mind, the rest are going to do whatever the supreme asshole tells them to do, and I broke the supreme asshole's nose."

The headstones said nothing. They never did, no matter how many times I spoke to them. Or rather, they said only what was necessary: Conrad Sane, January 7, 1945 – April 1, 2006; Evangeline Sane, March 8, 1956 – April 1, 2006. No matter what I said, that's all they said back.

"All because of a girl. You'd like Lily, though. I really think you would. She's fun and she's smart and she's way too good for me. And I fucked it up. Actually, I fucked everything up. I took something from her that I can't ever give back and then I broke her heart when she needed me. Clara's not speaking to me anymore. She's leaving because I disgust her. I broke my boss' nose. Well, my boss' boss' boss' nose. Now I'm about to lose my job. And here I am, talking to a pair of stones. I don't have anyone left to talk to, so I'm talking to a pair of fucking stones."

They left the after party around 1:30 in the morning. Who is on the road at 1:30 in the morning? Just my parents and the drunks, and the drunks can't drive so they slam into other cars at intersections because they don't know that they should stop or if they do they can't figure out which one's the brake pedal. The newspaper ran their obituaries alongside a review of my mother's last concert. The reviewer said it wasn't her best performance. I've never told them that. It seems a callous thing to tell someone who's dead. Then again, they've been pretty callous themselves.

"Six years and you haven't said anything to either of us. Well, fuck you, too."

That's the thing about talking to the dead. They never respond.

Chapter 14
The Hand That Feeds

Vespers District 1 Central Office main meeting room.

Enter Sane, Clara, Mengoweitz, the Board, Principal Hunter, Mr. Carter, and Community Members.

Sane and Clara sit at a wooden table near the front of the room facing a larger table where Mengoweitz, the Board, and Principal Hunter sit. Behind Sane and Clara are several rows of folding chairs, all occupied by Community Members. Mr. Carter sits against the western wall. A microphone is positioned in front of Sane and each member of the Board.

SANE *(to Clara)* What are you doing here?

CLARA I wasn't about to let the hounds tear apart my baby brother without his having proper representation.

SANE Proper representation?

CLARA You've retained my services as counsel.

SANE Oh yeah, this is going to go over real well.

Mengoweitz bangs his gavel.

MENGOWEITZ I call this hearing to order. Please rise. Mrs. Stephens?

STEPHENS I pledge allegiance to the Flag of the United States of America, and to the Republic for which it stands, one Nation under God, indivisible, with liberty and justice for all.

MENGOWEITZ Thank you. Mr. Slaren?

SLAREN Heavenly Father, please look with favor upon our proceedings. Guide our hands this day so that we can do the work necessary and accomplish ends in the best interests of all involved. In Your Son Christ Jesus' name, we pray. Amen.

MENGOWEITZ Thank you. Everyone may be seated. This hearing has been called to address the very serious allegations made against Julian Sane, English teacher at Vespers Community High School. Mr. Sane stands accused of moral turpitude. The charges assert that Mr. Sane utilized his position as a teacher to engage in sexual misconduct with a student, Miss Lily Carter, these past two months. Mr. Sane is also accused of assaulting the president of this board, Alastair Mengoweitz, who is I, at Dr. Mengoweitz' residence. Mr. Sane is further charged with harassment of board member Shirley Betts at Mrs. Betts' residence. Before we begin, Mr. Sane, would you identify the woman seated next to you?

SANE She's my bookie. I figure I better start playing the ponies since I'm about to be out of a job.

CLARA *(covering the microphone)* Julian, behave yourself.

MENGOWEITZ Mr. Sane, please remember where you are and conduct yourself appropriately.

SANE A thousand pardons, effendi.

MENGOWEITZ Who is seated at your table?

CLARA *(rising)* Clara Sane, sir. I am Mr. Sane's sister and I will be acting as defense counsel during this hearing.

MENGOWEITZ You're an attorney?

CLARA No.

MENGOWEITZ Then I'm afraid I'm going to have to ask you to join the gallery, Miss Sane.

CLARA Surely, you would not deny counsel to a man accused of such severe charges. What will the press think?

MENGOWEITZ Very well, but you are expected to conduct yourself, you and Mr. Sane, in a manner commensurate with this place and the sincerity of our proceedings.

Clara sits.

SANE Someone read his thesaurus this morning.

MENGOWEITZ Mr. Sane!

CLARA Damnit, Julian!

SANE I'm sorry. Please continue.

MENGOWEITZ Mr. Sane, regretfully, you are permitted to make an opening statement. Would you care to make such a statement at this time?

SANE Actually, I'd—

CLARA *(covering the microphone)* Julian, you need to garner sympathy from these people, from the board and the community. If you act like an asshole, you're not going to garner anything but contempt. Make a statement and be nice.

MENGOWEITZ Mr. Sane? We're waiting.

SANE *(rising)* Yes, sir. Sorry, sir. First off, allow me to apologize to Mrs. Betts for what she perceived as harassment. My intent was merely to discuss the matter at hand with her so as to enlighten her regarding my side. I sincerely apologize for any misunderstanding. Second, allow me to apologize to Dr. Mengoweitz for breaking his nose after he made a disparaging comment about my mother. Dr. Mengoweitz, you have the right to make whatever disparaging comments you wish about whomever you wish. My reaction was impulsive and I deeply regret not acting in a manner more befitting a civilized individual.

CLARA *(whispering)* Careful.

SANE With regards to the central reason for this hearing, I would like to say that I made a mistake, a serious misjudgment. I regret any embarrassment my actions have caused the district. For the record, I have ended my relationship with the lady in question. I would like to add that at the time our relationship began, she was not a student in the district, nor was she ever a student of mine. Thank you.

Sane sits.

MENGOWEITZ Before we continue, I'd like to remind everyone present that though temperatures are likely to run a bit hot, given the nature of this hearing, everyone is expected to remain quiet and respectful. Now then. The board members have a number of questions for you, Mr. Sane, to assess exactly how this situation arose. We will then turn to a number of witnesses who have information germane to our inquiry. We will then return to you, Mr. Sane, at which point the board will decide how to proceed.

SANE *(aside)* Gee, I wonder what their decision will be.

CLARA *(whispering)* Shut up.

MENGOWEITZ Mr. O'Neill, would you care to start?

O'NEILL Thank you. Mr. Sane, I wonder if you could start by telling us exactly when your relationship with Miss Carter began.

SANE Exactly?

CLARA One moment, please. *(covering the microphone)* Don't be cagey, Julian. Just tell them the truth.

SANE I'm not sure what the truth is.

CLARA Don't tell them that.

O'NEILL Mr. Sane?

CLARA *(to the Board)* Just a minute.

SANE *(to Clara)* It's okay. *(to the Board)* My relationship with Miss Carter began near the beginning of the summer, shortly after the high school's graduation.

O'NEILL Can you be more specific? Did it begin immediately after graduation? A few days later? A week or more after?

SANE We became reacquainted the day after graduation, but I'd say our relationship really began a few weeks later.

O'NEILL When you say you became reacquainted, what do you mean?

SANE I knew her when she was a student here, knew of her, that is, but I didn't have any contact with her in the intervening year between her graduation and this summer.

O'NEILL How would you characterize your relationship with Miss Carter during her years as a student at VCHS?

SANE I wouldn't call it a relationship at all. I knew who she was and what she looked like. That's about it.

O'NEILL That's about it or that's it?

SANE That's it. Who she was, what she looked like.

O'NEILL Tell me, Mr. Sane, are you in the habit of identifying students with whom you maintain no real relationship via their physical appearance, or was Miss Carter a special case?

SANE Due respect, how else am I supposed to tell them apart?

Laughter from the Community Members.

Mengoweitz pounds his gavel.

MENGOWEITZ Silence!

Clara *(whispering)* Watch it, Julian.

O'NEILL Fair enough. So, your claim is that you had no contact with Miss Carter prior to this summer?

SANE I may have had fleeting contact with her, but nothing of substance.

O'NEILL Okay. Skipping ahead to this summer. Can you tell us how you became reacquainted with Miss Carter?

SANE I was under the weather one day and we ran into each other. She escorted me back to my house to make sure I got there safely.

O'NEILL You were sick?

SANE Yes.

O'NEILL Stomach flu?

SANE No.

O'NEILL Cold?

SANE No.

164

O'NEILL What ailment were you suffering from?

SANE I think you mean, from what ailment were you suffering?

O'NEILL Mr. Sane, answer the question.

SANE I had been drinking. I drank a bit too much.

O'NEILL You were intoxicated.

SANE Yes.

O'NEILL Publically.

SANE Yes.

O'NEILL And Miss Carter escorted you home?

SANE Yes.

O'NEILL Did she drop you at your door?

SANE No.

O'NEILL What did she do, Mr. Sane?

SANE She took my keys, unlocked the door, and ushered me to my bed to sleep it off.

O'NEILL And did she leave?

SANE Yes.

O'NEILL Immediately?

A pause.

SANE No.

O'NEILL When did she leave, Mr. Sane?

SANE She left the following morning.

O'NEILL A student stayed the night in your house while you were intoxicated?

SANE If you're worried I violated her right then and there, I didn't. I was too drunk to do much of anything.

MENGOWEITZ It would be a mistake to make light of your situation, Mr. Sane.

SANE I'll keep that in mind.

O'NEILL Whose idea was it for Miss Carter to spend the night with you?

SANE Hers. She was worried about me and wanted to make sure I didn't choke to death on my own vomit in the middle of the night.

O'NEILL And thus you became reacquainted.

SANE Yes. Thus.

O'NEILL How romantic.

SANE Isn't it, though?

O'NEILL I have no further questions.

MENGOWEITZ Mr. Slaren?

SLAREN Thank you. Mr. Sane, I'd like to pick up where Mr. O'Neill left off. Can you explain how the two of you, yourself and Miss Carter, transitioned from that night of drunken debauchery to what you call your relationship?

SANE Yes.

Silence.

SLAREN Yes?

SANE Yes.

Silence.

CLARA *(covering the microphone)* What are you doing?

SANE He's being snotty, so I'm answering the exact question he asked.

CLARA Answer the question.

SANE *(to the Board)* She left her phone at my house. I arranged to meet her so I could return it. I tried to make it clear at that time that I had no interest in dating her, that I was uncomfortable with her having been in my house to begin with.

SLAREN Were you?

SANE Was I what?

SLAREN Were you uncomfortable with her having been in your house?

SANE Very much so. I thought it inappropriate.

SLAREN And yet here we are. What changed?

SANE Her car broke down in the middle of that last storm we had. She needed to get out of the rain, and I wasn't about to send her away with the weather being what it was, so she spent the night with me. Again.

166

SLAREN I assume you were not drunk that night.

SANE No.

SLAREN In what other ways was this night different?

SANE I think it was a different day of the week, for one.

SLAREN Mr. Sane.

SANE We stayed up most of the night playing board games and cards. Chess. That's about it.

SLAREN Was Miss Carter given alcohol to drink?

CLARA *(whispering)* Tell them I gave it to her.

SANE No.

CLARA They obviously already know she had it. Blame me.

A pause.

SANE *(to the Board)* She was freezing. Her clothing was soaked from the rain. My sister gave her a small drink while I found her some dry clothes.

SLAREN Mr. Sane, how old is Miss Carter?

SANE Nineteen.

SLAREN How old was she that night?

SANE Eighteen.

SLAREN What is the legal drinking age?

SANE Twenty-one.

SLAREN Is eighteen younger than twenty-one?

SANE Yes.

SLAREN So what you're saying is that you contributed to the delinquency of a minor, that you allowed alcohol to be given to someone you knew to be underage.

SANE Hey, Socrates made his students think. I say we discuss that for awhile.

SLAREN How many other students have you permitted alcohol be given to?

SANE None.

SLAREN How much do you yourself drink, Mr. Sane?

CLARA That is outrageous and has nothing to do with the topic of this hearing.

SLAREN Is your sister objecting because you drink excessively, Mr. Sane?

SANE I won't answer that.

SLAREN You will answer the question.

SANE No, I won't answer the question.

MENGOWEITZ Mr. Sane, you are expected to answer the questions put to you by this board.

SANE If they are relevant, I'll answer anything you want. I wear briefs, in case you were wondering.

SLAREN Mr. Sane, do you drink excessively? If you refuse to answer, we'll have to assume the answer is yes.

SANE Assume whatever the hell you want, but neither I nor my physician is going to answer that question. Move on.

Silence.

SLAREN Fine. How did your involvement with Miss Carter proceed after that night?

SANE We started exercising every morning in the park. We'd run laps together.

SLAREN Why?

SANE For the exercise.

SLAREN Why did you decide to take up an exercise regimen?

SANE I wanted to get in shape.

SLAREN For what reason?

SANE My health. Apparently, my blood pressure is a bit high.

SLAREN Was that your only reason?

SANE I came to enjoy the runs, if that's what you're asking.

SLAREN Mr. Sane, did you exercise with Miss Carter out of a desire to see her sweat?

SANE Nothing turns a man on quite like a sweaty, stinky female body. I'm going to need some alone time just thinking about it.

SLAREN I don't find your glibness nearly as amusing as you do.

SANE I'm devastated to hear that.

SLAREN Did you exercise with Miss Carter out of a desire to view her in a lascivious manner while maintaining the illusion that your intentions were nothing but pure?

SANE You lost me.

SLAREN Were you—

SANE I went running with Lily because I needed the exercise and because I enjoyed her company. Next question.

SLAREN You enjoyed her company. Can you tell us why?

SANE She kept me focused. I easily lose interest in things. I'm pretty sure it's pathological. I really should see someone about it. Can you recommend a therapist? Whoever you're seeing must be real good.

SLAREN You admit Miss Carter was a pleasant distraction for you?

SANE A distraction?

SLAREN You admit to using her.

SANE Is that what you heard? Is there a dead dung beetle with whom I can speak?

SLAREN Mr. Sane—

SANE No, you're done. Just shut up. You're done. I'm done with your stupidity. Just sit there. Next. *(to Stephens)* What do you have for me, Red?

STEPHENS I'm sorry?

MENGOWEITZ Go ahead, Mrs. Stephens.

STEPHENS Okay. Well. Mr. Sane, if you don't mind, I would like to finish out my colleagues questions regarding the initial stage of your relationship with Miss Carter.

SANE Okay, but only if you say please.

STEPHENS *(amused)* Please, Mr. Sane.

SANE But of course. Go ahead.

STEPHENS How did your morning exercise become more than routine exercise?

SANE Over time, we became fond of each other. You spend enough time in the company of another person, you're bound to grow fond of her. It wasn't something either one of us was pushing for.

STEPHENS How serious would you say the relationship was at this point?

169

A pause.

SANE I'm sorry. I'm not sure I understand the question.

STEPHENS You've dated women casually in the past, yes?

SANE Yes.

STEPHENS Okay. Would you characterize the relationship at this point as casual?

SANE Of course. Everything's casual until it's not. I didn't fall in love with her the moment our eyes first met, if that's what you mean. It wasn't serious until it was.

STEPHENS Mr. Sane, before I ask my next question, I would like to state for the record that I was not in favor of this hearing and that I do not believe your personal life to be necessarily anyone's business but your own.

SANE I understand.

STEPHENS Mr. Sane, at this point, before your relationship became serious, did you consider the appropriateness of such a relationship?

A pause.

SANE Yes, I did.

STEPHENS You did?

SANE Yes.

STEPHENS And?

SANE And I decided to pursue it. I wanted to see where it would lead.

STEPHENS Did you consider the repercussions of such a relationship?

SANE Abstractly, yes.

STEPHENS Abstractly?

SANE I knew it would not ingratiate me to anyone, but I didn't anticipate anything like this.

STEPHENS You never considered it would cost you your status in the community, possibly your job and your career?

SANE Not like this, no. Like I said, I expected my decision to be unpopular, but nothing like this.

STEPHENS I see. One last question, if you'll permit me. What is the current status of your relationship with Miss Carter?

SANE We broke up.

STEPHENS May I ask who initiated the break-up?

SANE I did.

STEPHENS Why?

SANE I felt under the circumstances she'd be better off.

STEPHENS I see. Thank you very much for your time.

MENGOWEITZ At this point, I know the board members still have a number of questions for you regarding your relationship, but before we continue with those, I would like to hear from two other people who have been entangled in this situation. Principal Madeline Hunter?

HUNTER Yes, sir.

MENGOWEITZ Good evening. We're glad you could be here tonight. We only have a few questions for you, but we would appreciate any insight you might be able to share.

HUNTER Of course.

MENGOWEITZ Can you start by telling us your relationship to Mr. Sane.

HUNTER I'm his building principal.

MENGOWEITZ You're his boss.

HUNTER Yes.

MENGOWEITZ His immediate superior.

HUNTER Yes.

MENGOWEITZ How did you first learn of his relationship with Miss Carter?

HUNTER I heard a rumor in a number of places and a number of times, always his name in conjunction with hers.

MENGOWEITZ And what did you do when you heard this rumor?

HUNTER Initially, I ignored it. There will always be rumors in a small town. I can't take every single one of them seriously.

MENGOWEITZ But at some point, you decided to take this one seriously?

HUNTER Yes. Not long after the rumors began, I was contacted by a member of the board and asked if it was speculation or if there was something to it.

MENGOWEITZ Which board member was it who asked?

HUNTER You did.

MENGOWEITZ How did you proceed?

HUNTER I went to Mr. Sane's home and inquired for myself.

MENGOWEITZ And what did he say?

HUNTER He said it was none of my business and told me to leave.

MENGOWEITZ Is that how he said it?

HUNTER He was a bit cruder than that, but basically.

MENGOWEITZ What were his exact words?

A pause.

HUNTER He told me to get the fuck off his property.

MENGOWEITZ And did he admit to his relationship with Miss Carter?

HUNTER Eventually, yes.

MENGOWEITZ What did he say?

HUNTER He confirmed that they were seeing each other.

MENGOWEITZ Is that how he put it?

A pause.

HUNTER He was very frustrated with me and my intrusive questions.

MENGOWEITZ What did he say, Mrs. Hunter?

HUNTER He said he was fucking her anywhere and anytime he could.

MENGOWEITZ He said that?

HUNTER Yes.

MENGOWEITZ Did you ask him to stop seeing her?

HUNTER Yes, I did. He did not respond positively.

MENGOWEITZ Was this the only time you spoke with Mr. Sane regarding this matter?

HUNTER No. He came to my office a few days later to discuss things further.

MENGOWEITZ Had his attitude improved at all?

HUNTER No. I informed him of this hearing and of the possibility of his dismissal. This, understandably, angered him.

MENGOWEITZ Principal Hunter, in his anger, did Mr. Sane attack you personally, either verbally or physically?

A pause.

HUNTER Yes. Verbally.

MENGOWEITZ What did he say?

HUNTER He referred to me with a very disgusting epithet.

MENGOWEITZ He called you a name?

HUNTER Yes.

MENGOWEITZ What did he call you?

A pause.

HUNTER *(quietly)* A fucking cunt.

MENGOWEITZ I'm sorry. Could you repeat that?

HUNTER *(louder)* A fucking cunt.

MENGOWEITZ There was some noise there. Could you repeat that one more time?

HUNTER *(clearly and forcefully)* He called me a fucking cunt.

SANE In hindsight, I do feel really bad about that, Maddy. Sorry.

HUNTER In his defense—

MENGOWEITZ *(interrupting)* Thank you, Mrs. Hunter. You may be seated.

HUNTER In his defense—

MENGOWEITZ *(interrupting)* Thank you, Mrs. Hunter.

HUNTER In Mr. Sane's defense—

MENGOWEITZ *(frustrated, interrupting)* Tha—

HUNTER *(interrupting)* Please allow me to finish. You asked me a question and I would like to give a complete and full response to it. Now either let me finish answering or the next hearing you have will be regarding my behavior. In Mr. Sane's defense, he was very angry. He was hurt and betrayed. While I personally believe his actions are in an ethically gray area, an area I would much rather have had him avoid entirely, they were actions and decisions made by two consenting adults. As much as I may not like it, it was never my place to interfere.

MENGOWEITZ Are you saying you condone his actions?

HUNTER No. I'm saying I was a fucking cunt. He was right in that it's none of my business.

MENGOWEITZ Thank you for your illuminating comments, Mrs. Hunter. I would now like to hear from Florian Carter. Mr. Carter?

CARTER Yes, sir.

MENGOWEITZ Mr. Carter, would you state your relationship to Miss Carter?

CARTER Lily's my daughter. My only child.

MENGOWEITZ Do you love your daughter?

CARTER More than anything in the world.

MENGOWEITZ Were you aware of your daughter's relationship with Mr. Sane?

CARTER Yes, I was. I met him the night of their first date. Introduced himself all proper to me.

MENGOWEITZ Were you accepting of his dating your daughter?

CARTER I never had a problem with it.

MENGOWEITZ Were you aware that Mr. Sane was once your daughter's teacher?

SANE *(jumping to his feet)* No, she wasn't! She was never my student!

CLARA Julian, sit down!

SANE *(to Clara)* No! *(to Mengoweitz)* I don't care if you try to cut my balls off, but you're going to tell the goddamn truth! I was a teacher in the building Lily attended. I was never her teacher!

Silence.

CARTER That was my understanding, as well, sir. Mr. Sane was not actually her teacher. Even if he had been, I really wouldn't have cared. She graduated. She's a grown woman. She can date whoever she wants.

Sane sits.

MENGOWEITZ Mr. Carter, given the situation that's developed as a result of their relationship, can you really tell me you still approve of it?

CARTER They don't have a relationship now. Which does kinda piss me off. *(to Sane)* Mr. Sane, if I wasn't a civilized man, I'd break both your legs. Lily laid up in her old room crying for three straight days. You made my little girl cry, Mr. Sane. That ain't right.

SANE I didn't mean to hurt your daughter.

CARTER But you did.

SANE I did what I thought was best for her at the time. I didn't want to hurt her.

Silence.

MENGOWEITZ Mr. Carter, thank you for your time.

CLARA *(whispering)* You might actually pull through this intact.

SANE *(quietly)* I'm done, Clara.

MENGOWEITZ Mr. Sane, I would like to return to you now.

SANE *(rising)* No. We're done.

MENGOWEITZ Mr. Sane, we're done when I say we're done. Sit down.

SANE No, we're done now. I went along with this farce under the delusion that I'd come out unscathed, and for what? Florian here has more beef with me than any of you. I made his little girl cry. Why did I do this? Because of you, because of this kangaroo court you've assembled to persecute me. All this because I fell in love with a woman. Jesus Christ, what would you have done if I had fallen in love with a man? Or if I had converted to Islam? And because I got scared, I broke the heart of the woman I love. I broke it into a thousand tiny pieces and made a bloody heap at my feet. Then I kicked it away. Because I knew that was the only way I could keep her away from this. Or, at least, I thought that would. What happened, Alastair? Did she come to you or did you go to her? Did you try to comfort her in her distress at all, or did you jump right into pumping her for information like some kind of emotional rapist?

I'm not sure what I could say to you, to this glorious inquisition you've assembled, that would have any bearing on your decision.

MENGOWEITZ *(interrupting)* Mr. Sane, are you finished?

SANE No, I'm not finished, but interrupt me again and I'll break more than just your nose. I fell in love with a woman. God strike me down! I fell in love with a woman! Oh, I never got to tell her that, thanks to you. *(pauses)* What right did any of you have to interfere with my personal life?

MENGOWEITZ This board is charged with protecting that which every parent in this community holds dearest.

SANE And this is how you do it? You attack a teacher for dating a woman? A grown woman. A woman capable of making her own decisions.

MENGOWEITZ A woman who once looked to you as a mentor, as a guide.

SANE I barely knew her when she was a student, and even if I had known her, what is the real harm in that? Do you really believe my dating Lily is going to lead to teachers having sexual relationships with their actual students? That does happen, and it should be prosecuted when it does. But that is not what happened here. What happened here was, two adults entered into a relationship of their own volition.

MENGOWEITZ You violated the trust she put in you.

Silence.

SANE Yes, I did. You're absolutely right. I violated her trust the moment I broke up with her because some irrelevant asshole didn't like us dating and decided to make a big stink about it. I will apologize to her for that. And I will apologize to Florian for making his daughter cry. And I will apologize to Principal Hunter for calling her what I did. None of that was called for. But I will not apologize to you for falling in love with her. I will not beg your forgiveness, I will not seek your absolution, because I did nothing wrong. Go ahead and fire me. I am through playing this game with you.

MENGOWEITZ You're fired, Mr. Sane. This is hearing is adjourned.

Mengoweitz bangs his gavel.

CLARA Shit. Well, that happened.

Chapter 15
Release All Light

The board members left first. Most of them avoided so much as looking in my direction. One of them went so far as to feign fascination with the sterile office architecture. The supreme asshole was the only one to look me in the eyes. He sneered as best as his smashed face would allow, and I let him. I'd said my part. Anything more would have been petty. Madeline—she wasn't my boss anymore—clapped a hand on my shoulder and squeezed. Her eyes were all puffy and red. If she wanted to say anything, she didn't, which was probably best for both of us. What did we have to say to each other? Either she understood or she didn't, and if she didn't understand, she never would.

Everyone else—community members, faculty members, students—got to their feet and exited without a word. They made no sound except for the occasional squeak of a soft spot beneath the carpeting and the metallic whine of the door hinges. There was no heckling, no commentary of any kind, no real sense that anyone had gotten what he wanted or was particularly pleased with the outcome. It was just over. Blame had been assigned, justice meted out, and order restored. The bad man who had violated a child had been exposed for the monster he was. All was right with the world.

Clara sat beside me until the door hinges gave a last whine and then were silent, and then she put an arm around my neck and hugged me as tight as the awkward position would allow. She had been right, she knew she had been right, and yet she had come to stand right beside me as the bombs fell. There would be no saying she told me so, no blame shifting, no pointless squabbling. There would be this embrace, this warm and loving embrace in lieu of absolutely nothing, followed by a long car ride, then drinks and perhaps a simple meal, and then we would retire for the night knowing that each of us would still be there in the morning when we woke.

The door hinges whined and the floor creaked under a hurried pair of feet. The reporter, Jamie Whoever, came toward us tape recorder in hand. She brandished it, but feebly, as if she didn't really want or expect any responses to her questions. She asked this and that, the usual questions for a fluff piece that would bear no relation to the truth. Neither of us said anything to her. Eventually, she dropped the hand holding out the tape recorder, smiled, wished us a pleasant evening, and left. Clara would later tell me that of all the articles and editorials run about my hearing, that reporter's was the only one to portray me in any kind of positive light and the only one to mention Madeline and Florian's attempted defenses.

I suggested we leave and drink ourselves silly. Clara rose from her seat but said I needed to go outside and face the world alone. Maybe that had been my problem all along. When had I actually stood on my own two feet? When had I not been leaning on Clara or Madeline or the board or even Lily? Whatever awaited me outside those doors awaited me, not me and whatever cane I found conveniently at hand. I could face it or I could hide behind someone's skirt. I could drink until my liver disintegrated. I could snort my bank account away and fuck every piece of willing ass from here to California. I could run away or I could stand.

Outside, two birds on a power line kept watching each other. A pair of drifters pushed shopping carts filled with plastic bags and cans down the sidewalk. The last few of those who had attended the hearing got into their cars and drove away to their own lives. A squirrel dashed through the parking lot and scampered up an oak tree whose branches shaded the entrance.

Silhouetted against a patch of virgin sky: Lily Carter.

"Hey."

She looked down at her feet, at a row of cars, at the drifters watching the two of us, then at me. "Hey."

"I got myself fired."

"I saw." When I didn't respond, she added, "I was sitting in the back. Figured you should have someone besides your sister there for you."

"Oh." Silence. "Thanks."

"Yeah. Well."

I looked up at the darkening sky, at the first faint stars glittering against a growing blackness.

"So what are you going to do now?" she asked.

"I haven't really thought about it. Maybe I'll go back to school, get my PhD. I hear colleges are pretty accepting of this sort of thing."

She thought for a minute. "Julian Sane. Professor Sane. Doctor Sane."

"Something like that. Maybe I'll write a memoir about us, about this summer."

I meant it as a joke, but Lily's face darkened. "I don't think that would be a good idea."

"I could set the record straight."

"Why?"

I didn't respond.

"I'm sorry you lost your job."

"Me too."

She turned away, then turned back and kissed me hard on the mouth with closed lips. "Thank you," she said.

"For what?"

"A girl always remembers her first time. How many girls can look back and say it really was everything it was supposed to be?"

"Lily—"

"Don't start."

A gust of wind lifted her hair into skeins like black smoke and I understood what I hadn't at the time. I brushed the strands from her eyes, trailed my fingers along the curve of her cheek, cupped her face in my hand, felt the soft glow of her skin beneath my thumb. Lily closed her eyes and rubbed her face into my palm, the once familiar glint of a smile crossing her lips. I let my hand fall to her shoulder and down her arm.

"I don't care what happened afterwards," I said. "I'd do it all again."

She kissed my cheek and then wiped away whatever was beneath our eyes. "Me too."

I took her into my arms, and she held me like she did once before— before the rumor and the gossip, before the accusations, before the trial— when there was no one else but two people making fools of themselves for each other's delight. It was the last dance of the ball, that moment when the orchestra winds down and yet you pray for one last extended coda before the doors open and the outside world intrudes. There was no snow to mark the occasion, no great downpour from the heavens, no shower of cherry blossoms. We held each other tight as we swayed from side to side to a song only the two of us could hear.

And in my head, we never left. We're still swaying in that parking lot, swaying, swaying.

THE END

From *WGMP News At Six*, August 12, 2012

Anchor: "In local news, high school teacher Julian Sane has been dismissed from his position following allegations of sexual misconduct with a former student. Sane went before the school board in an open meeting to answer the allegations last night after weeks of community outrage. A representative for both the school board and the district stated that, quote, Teachers like Mr. Sane do irreparable harm to the reputations of hard-working teachers everywhere. Firing Mr. Sane was the only proper course of action, end quote. Though a small minority has called Sane's hearing a witch-hunt, the general community seems pleased with its outcome. In other news, two teenagers are under investigation for stealing a car and subsequently driving it into the Wabash River. The two boys, whose names have not yet been released to the public, allegedly stole an Aston Martin belonging to physician Alastair Mengoweitz outside of Vespers General Hospital. Police have not spoken about the boys' involvement, but sources close to the investigation have told WGMP that, when questioned, both boys said, quote, He paid us to do it, end quote. No charges have been filed. Dr. Mengoweitz could not be reached for comment."

Jonathan M. Cook was born in 1982. He attended Eastern Illinois University where he received an MA in Literature. He currently lives in Robinson, IL.

www.ingramcontent.com/pod-product-compliance
Lightning Source LLC
Chambersburg PA
CBHW071241130626
46556CB00003B/1106